Chicken

Chicken

PAULA
MARTINAC

Bella
BOOKS
Ferndale, Michigan
2001

Bella Books, Inc.
P.O. Box 201007
Ferndale, MI 48220

Printed in the United States of America on acid-free paper
First Bella Books Edition
    The first edition of *Chicken* was published by Alyson
Publications in 1997.

Cover designer: Bonnie Liss (Phoenix Graphics)

ISBN 1-931513-07-4

To Katie, for staring

Ah, trouble, trouble,
there are two different kinds…
there's the one you give
and the other you take.

—*Kay Boyle*

Protect me from what I want.

—*Jenny Holzer*

For a while I stopped answering my phone.

I know that doesn't seem so interesting or unusual on the face of it. I live in New York City, where probably 90 percent of the middle class doesn't answer the phone. But *I* was never like that. People used to be amazed that I actually picked up. I liked catching callers in the act of thinking that I wasn't home, that they could just leave a message on my machine. Phone cowards, I called them. I'd pick up, and they'd sputter and try to recover their composure without letting on that they really, *really* thought they were just going to leave a twenty-second message and be done with it. No, I stymied their plans by forcing them to talk to a living, breathing, responsive person. I was such a self-righteous phone-answering snob.

But then I became just like everyone else. It wasn't that I didn't pick up because I was in the shower or eating dinner or in the middle of some brilliant thought that I didn't want to interrupt. No, I actually hovered over the machine with the sound turned up like someone with nothing better to do, listening to the message even as it was being left, turning down the volume on voices that I didn't want to hear. Sometimes, if it was a friend like Harold or Beth, I considered picking up the receiver in the middle of the message, but I never did — too afraid to admit that I'd been hovering, screening the world out. The beauty of it was, I'd spent so many years taking all my calls that no one believed I'd do anything else. When I stopped answering the phone, my friends just reached the conclusion that I was wildly busy with my two torrid love affairs.

"Out again, Miss Lynnie?" was Harold's usual message. "Those two young things are keeping somebody *mighty busy*, aren't they? You chicken hawk, you." I hated his tone; it had this creepy, sexual voyeurism to it. That's why I didn't pick up. "I'm pea green. It must be tough. Call me, kiddo, when you get a *chance*."

"Lynn, are you there?" That was Beth. "No, of course you're not; you're never there. I *never* see you anymore." With Beth I couldn't stand the guilt she tried to lay on me. "I miss you. I'll try you during the day tomorrow, but you never seem to be around *then* either."

Little did they know that I wasn't in the throes of passion when they called me at home, that I was actually hiding out in a way. Because my life got a little out of control. It started spinning, if you want to know the truth, like the earth gone crazy and defying the laws of nature. When I was a little kid, I used to wonder how the earth *knew* just exactly how fast to spin, so that nobody fell off because it was going too slowly or was pitched off because it was going too fast. My life started to feel like a globe that didn't know its own speed or was being twirled maniacally by some big hand, faster and faster and faster. And there I was, digging into the dirt with my fingers, trying desperately to stay on but not having a rat's chance. Then I didn't know what to do anymore to survive, so I just jumped off and started watching everybody spin and spin without me.

Now this metaphor is out of control. The bottom line is, I stopped answering the phone because the whole miserable situation with my young paramours, Lexy and Jude, which I'm about to explain to you, just about did me in.

I should have known by their names. Lexy. And Jude. Neither one is short for anything; those are just their names. There's a whole new generation of women who aren't called Lynn or Beth or Kathy anymore. When my friend Beth was pregnant with her daughter, she asked me to look at a baby-name book with her one night. Her husband, Paul, insisted that he didn't care what the baby was called, as long as it wasn't Beth Jr. or Paul II. "Let's not be total narcissists, okay?" was the way he put it. Beth's *What's in a Name Book* was published in 1993, and the twenty most recommended names for girls — based on what the authors called "grace, originality, and class" — included Vanessa, Angelica, Chrysta, and Zoe. Lynn and Beth, which used to be as common as rotary phones and typewriters, had become as outdated as Gladys and Evelyn were when I was growing up.

"Face it, we're old," said Beth, a forty-year-old baby boomer who'd made a career first instead of children. "We're the Ethels of our generation." Against my advice Beth named her daughter Alice Rose after the baby's two great-grandmothers, even though I told her the kid would have a rough time in school with a name like that.

"Alice is a classic," Beth insisted. But I notice she calls the baby "Ali," maybe to appease the name gods of the 1990s.

Back to Lexy and Jude. I remember asking my future girlfriends a variation on the same question: "Lexy — is that short for Alexis or Alexandra?" and "Jude — is that short for Judith?" but coming up with a "no" reply each time.

3

Lexy, it turned out, was conceived on Lexington Avenue in Manhattan in 1973, if you can believe that it's possible for someone to have been born in the 1970s and now walk, talk, hold a job, and have sex. "Just a few blocks north of Bloomingdale's," she pointed out.

"Lucky they didn't call you Bloomie," I noted, but I was the only one who thought it was funny.

You've probably already guessed that Jude's parents were die-hard Beatles fans, true to the Fab Four even after the breakup of the band. Jude, born in 1971, didn't share their musical taste. In fact, she claims never to have heard the song "Hey Jude" in its entirety. "Too boring," she said. "All those na-na-na-nas." I'm glad I didn't bother to tell her that the Beatles were my *life* when I was growing up. To Jude the Beatles were simply Paul McCartney's first band.

I'm not sure what I was thinking when I started "seeing" first Lexy, then Jude. I prided myself on being so levelheaded, so sure of myself, so in touch with my feelings, so mature. After all, I answered my phone, didn't I? I didn't play the games that other people did. I had a good job; a homey, comfortable, rent-stabilized apartment in New York; and funny, bright friends who knew that Neil Young had a career before the movie *Philadelphia* ever came out. I had been in a serious, stable, monogamous relationship for thirteen years.... Well, that's it, then, isn't it? That's when this nightmare started, when Claire left.

After we broke up I didn't want to keep in touch with Claire. I didn't see myself as one of those lesbians who could stand to have an army of ex-lovers of whom I could say proudly, "Oh, we broke up years ago, and we're so much better as friends." I know I'm going to seem petty and vindictive, but I didn't want to be friends with some-

4

one who gave up on us after thirteen years, stating as her excuse that she didn't think we were "enlarging ourselves" anymore.

"What does that mean?" I asked, looking around for something convenient to throw. But we were standing on a street corner — Astor Place and Lafayette, to be exact; we'd just been to an incomprehensible play at the Public Theater — and the only things available were a trash can and the rat that was scurrying away from it. "How should we be 'enlarging ourselves'? I've already outgrown everything I owned that was a size eight."

She didn't laugh, and I knew I was in trouble. I could always make Claire laugh. It was one of the bases on which our relationship was founded, I realized later — my ability to deliver clever one-liners and quips, and her ability to laugh at them, even when she was feeling blue. "We should be expanding our interests, learning new things, meeting new people," she said with a wispy sigh that blew out in a little cloud. "We don't learn from each other anymore, the way we used to."

"We've been busy," I said, always a fast thinker. "We've just got to stop and make time for each other. I swear that time has been speeding up — don't you think? — since we both turned forty. I mean, a day now is really only about an hour long."

Another joke that fell flat on its face. I don't think she was really even listening to me at that point. She was just standing with her hands twisting around in her coat pockets as if she were keeping some important secret in them.

"Look, why are we doing this on the street?" I asked. "Can't we go home and discuss this?" It wasn't that I was afraid that people were looking at us, which they were. I've had numerous fights with Claire and other people on the streets of New York. Public fighting is kind of liberating, knowing you have the whole sidewalk and all the airspace above the buildings to fill up with your shouting. And when you get really into a good fight, you don't even notice the way total strangers turn to stare at you as they pass by, privy to your most intimate thoughts and problems.

I suggested going home because I was hoping I could ward off her saying the inevitable words "I'm going to move out." If I could just get her into our cozy little apartment, so squeezed with the memorabilia of thirteen years, she'd realize that she couldn't leave. "Oh, there's the chair we dragged home from First Avenue and refinished." "There's the picture of us kissing on Valentine's Day in 1985, just after we promised we'd be together forever." "There are the candleholders your mother gave us the year she stopped praying you'd find a husband and finally saw us as a couple."

But Claire wasn't having any of my all-too-transparent ploy of trying to get her back to our home. After thirteen years, what don't couples know about each other? — except, incredibly, that one person is so unhappy she has to leave.

"I can't," she said simply. "I know this sounds ridiculous, coming so suddenly, but I just can't. I'm going to call Beth and see if I can stay with her and Paul tonight."

Beth? *My* friend Beth? It took a minute for me to remember that, of course, Beth was Claire's friend before she was mine, so she had first dibs on her; they'd known each other since college. What would Claire tell Beth about me to poison our friendship? Not only was I going to have to let go of Claire but it looked as if I was going to start losing friends too.

But maybe there was another way to see it. Maybe Beth, who was a cherished friend to us both, would talk to Claire about her hasty decision. Maybe she'd make her see that thirteen years is not something to throw away lightly on a street corner.

"That's a good idea," I allowed about the plan to sleep at Beth's. "Let's spend a night apart and think things through. Things will seem clearer tomorrow." I sounded like Scarlett O'Hara, putting off until tomorrow the breakup that was actually taking place today.

"Yeah," she agreed. She started to walk south, the wrong direction for Beth and Paul's place on Tenth Street and for our apartment in the East Twenties. Even as my stomach was sinking, my mind wildly accusing, "There's someone else, she's lying to me, she's going to her right now," Claire turned abruptly and started north with an embarrassed smile. "I...I'm a little disoriented, I guess," she said.

"Let me walk you," I offered, but she shook her hand at me over her shoulder and walked away.

That was how it happened with Claire after thirteen years, and that was when I started smoking again after almost as many years without so much as a puff. It was automatic. It wasn't as if I thought about it — "Gee, I'd love to have a cigarette right now." I just walked right over to a deli on Broadway and up to the counter and said, as I had said a million times in earlier years, "A pack of Marlboros, please."

Of course, there's a lot more that happened with Claire that I'm not interested in rehashing right now. The truth is, my behavior wasn't very pretty. Spurned lovers aren't the most gracious or sensible people. I'm not proud that some of Claire's things were mysteriously destroyed, like her grandmother's Spode cup that was Claire's favorite for drinking tea in the morning and just wasn't the same without its handle. Or the comforting, oversized, black wool sweater that she wore every winter weekend until she found that someone (namely me) had unraveled it to the length of a bolero jacket. I admit it — Claire's leaving made me want to act more like a pouty ten-year-old than the mature adult I claimed to be.

The other thing that I'll mention, just to get it out in the open, is that, yes, I was a bit of a stalker. I never knew these things about myself and my personality until Claire left, because no one had ever rejected me before. I'd always been the one to call it quits, the one in my impetuous youth — the time I call "Before Claire" — who had one foot out of the bed.

After Claire found her own apartment in Brooklyn, she handed me the address and phone number on a slip of paper, which I vindictively crumpled right before her eyes and threw into the trash can. "And you wonder," she remarked bitterly, "why I'm going." Later I fished the paper out of the trash and signed her up for a few magazine subscriptions I knew would annoy her — *Modern Bride, Playgirl, Car and Driver* — and added her to the mailing list of Operation Rescue. I memorized her phone number and would call it late at night just to see if she was home. When I heard her say "Hello," I'd hang up, tormenting both of us. After a few weeks, a recorded message from NYNEX came on informing me that, at the customer's request, the phone number had been changed and was, at the customer's request, unlisted. I listened to the recording a couple of times, then hung up, sad and mortified beyond belief.

The words to an old song that had never made sense to me when I was a kid inexplicably popped into my mind: "You Always Hurt the One You Love." My dad had a favorite recording of it by the Mills Brothers, who crooned it in a smooth, upbeat, jazzy tempo that didn't match its sentiment. Dad played it over and over. The gist of the song was that no matter how hard you try not to, you always end up "crushing" your lover into a pathetic heap. But the pain you inflict only shows how much you really, really care. Poor Claire, getting involved with someone who'd had it drummed into her subconscious at an impres-

8

sionable age that hurting someone else was a zippy, happy, swinging thing to do.

I know I confessed how I started smoking again. But did I mention my drinking? Probably not. It was my least favorite of "Things I Discovered About Myself" After Claire. I'd never really been a drinker before. Claire and I might each have a beer on a Saturday night or, on special occasions, a glass of wine. I was so much *not* a drinker that more than one of anything made me start to giggle and go cottony in the head. Claire had a slightly higher tolerance for alcohol and used to make fun of me for getting drunk so fast. If we were at a restaurant or party, she'd quip, "I guess I'm the designated driver" and steer me quickly into a cab so we could get home fast.

When Claire left, I found my social world had collapsed around me, even though I still had friends. Thirteen years with one person and I didn't know what to do with myself anymore, especially on weekends. Claire and I had gone to movies almost every Friday night as a way to unwind from the week, but I didn't know how to enjoy movies on my own. There was no one to share a tub of popcorn and a large Coke with. There was no one to poke and whisper, "I *love* this" or "Isn't this *terrible?*" to. And worst of all, Friday was a big date night. Trying movies solo, I'd sit on the aisle and put my coat or bag on the seat next to mine, the one where Claire had always sat, and I'd pretend my companion was perpetually in the bathroom. At first even I believed it, and I'd look around anxiously for Claire to come down the aisle. Then "Is that seat taken?" a straight man would invariably ask, and, humiliated, I'd have to relinquish the place to him and his date.

Solo Friday nights at the movies went by the wayside pretty fast. It was Harold who took pity on me and asked if I wanted him to accompany me to P.J.'s one Friday night. "I'm not sure I could survive the Clit Club," he joked, fanning himself. "I'm just a poor little virgin."

"Oh, right," I said, rolling my eyes. But I didn't feel strong enough for the Clit Club either, the biggest lesbian cruising scene in the tristate area, so I let him off the hook. We met instead at P.J.'s, a small neighborhood spot that had been predominantly gay for about forty years, though it had had various names and incarnations. It had the kind of massive carved mahogany bar that distinguishes old New York bars, and the atmosphere was much more my speed: 33 rpm, just like my dad's Mills Brothers record. We could sit in P.J.'s for hours and have a beer or two and pretend all we were doing was having a beer or two and not trying to piece together a social life for me.

The thing is, it was the "or two" that presented a problem for me. Claire and I could stop at one because we didn't tend to hang out in bars for any length of time; we didn't need or want to. But Harold and I were making an evening of it, and it's hard to justify taking up table space nursing the same warm Heineken all night long.

So we ordered another round from a cute young thing with creamy skin, long auburn hair, a thin gold nose ring, and midnight blue nails who was wearing a black leather vest and low-slung black jeans with a change apron tied securely around her slim waist. The second beer made me ask her, "Aren't you cold with just that vest on?" and glance suggestively at the flimsy snaps that kept it from popping off.

"It's stuffy in here," she said with a coy smile. "It keeps me from getting, you know, overheated."

I returned the smile and gave her a two-dollar tip on an eight-dollar tab. "Go girl," Harold said, clinking his beer bottle against mine. "I see you're not going to need as many lessons as I thought you would." The next beers we drank were courtesy of Lexy, our little leather dyke.

After that night I started inviting other friends to P.J.'s on the weekends. One Saturday when no one was available, I swallowed my fear and trekked there on my own. It was just a few blocks from where I lived (where *we* had lived together) and a convenient stumble home, so it didn't really matter if I had one beer or four. There was no one to tease me about being a silly drunk, and my building was easy to find, even when I was foggy-headed. One Gay Pride weekend, my friends and upstairs neighbors, Jonathan and Alec, had strung a rainbow flag from their fire escape, and they had never bothered to take it down. "Every day should be Gay Pride Day" was the slogan Jonathan coined. Whenever the buildings on my block started to blur together, I could just look up and see Jonathan and Alec's flag and know I was home.

I know this all seems skewed, kind of like stepping into a time warp. After all, the '90s are supposed to be the time when the alcoholics get sober, not when the sober people turn into alcoholics. But I convinced myself that drinking all those beers at P.J.'s helped me, that it boosted my courage when I needed it most. It made it possible to play the part — Lynn Woods, the sophisticated, worldly-wise, forty-year-old freelance professional writer — that Claire's leaving had poked a big hole in. Take it from me: It's hard to feel sexy and desirable when you've not only been left but you're suddenly almost twice as old as everyone around you.

Lexy worked Friday and Saturday nights to supplement her

$16,000-a-year photo research assistant job at Time-Life. She was saving the money from her moonlighting so she could go to NYU graduate school in film. Her aspiration was to translate Sarah Schulman's Lower East Side novels onto the big screen. "They're so *real,* you know? The Lower East Side is just so…real."

Lexy had boundless energy that had nothing to do with artificial stimulants. She seemed to like talking to me, but I couldn't tell at first if it was just for the lavish 25- or 30-percent tips I left or because she was genuinely interested in me. I decided to take a chance and find out.

"Oh, I don't drink," she said when I offered to buy her something when she got off work. She said it not with disdain but almost with boredom, as if drinking were profoundly uninteresting. Still, the rejection stung hard and made me want to snap in defense, "I *wasn't* coming on to you," which, in fact, I managed to convince myself. I left P.J.'s earlier than usual that night, completely sober, and the next weekend made other plans.

Beth and Paul asked me to go to a performance piece in the East Village. The performer was an FTM transsexual, a man who had once been a woman who had identified as a lesbian. His lover, a lesbian who had been with him prior to his surgery, was now freaked-out and leaving him because she wanted a girlfriend, not a boyfriend. The piece was all about the transsexual's angst at realizing his relationship had sort of self-destructed. It was complicated to follow, but what was really hard was when he started to stick himself with pins, right onstage, to illustrate how he had become alienated from his own pain. I'm squeamish about things like that, and I felt a rush of sweat down my back. I stepped outside the cramped theater for air. Beth sent Paul to check that I hadn't fainted.

12

"You okay?"

"It's so stuffy in there," I said, sitting on the front steps of the performance space ripping off my vest.

"Yeah," he agreed, taking a place on the step beside me, "and the material's intense too." Paul is one of these nice, soft, well-meaning straight men who seem to have taken classes in sensitivity and self-awareness. He almost never lapsed from nonsexist language. He assumed from the first moment Beth knew she was pregnant that they would both have to make career sacrifices to raise the baby, which he hoped was a girl. You see what I mean.

There was one thing about him that struck me as odd, though. Before he met Beth, who is seven years older, he'd had a string of bad luck: two relationships in succession ended abruptly when the women came out as lesbians. When he found out Beth had once had an affair with a woman in college, their budding romance was almost pruned. Beth never told me or Claire what she said to Paul to hold on to him, probably because it would embarrass her to admit to two lesbians that she'd taken some kind of heterosexual loyalty oath.

"I can't go back in," I admitted to Paul, feeling a wave of nausea ebb and flow inside me at the memory of the pins sticking out of the performer's flesh. "You go ahead."

"Nah, the piece isn't very well written," he said. "You want me to get you some seltzer or water? A ginger ale?"

"Ginger ale," I said weakly. "That would be great."

Beth popped outside just as Paul was walking off for the ginger ale. "You okay?"

"Yeah, just a little queasy," I said. "You know me and *sharp* things."

"I know," Beth said. "Besides, the piece wasn't very well written."

I lit up a Marlboro to calm myself, even though I knew Beth disapproved of my newly regained habit. She moved away from me on purpose and started waving her hand dramatically in front of her to deflect the smoke, the way aggressive nonsmokers do to let you know what a health hazard you are.

"So," I said bravely, "how's you-know-who?"

I'd asked this question many times over the last months, and Beth was usually evasive, saying she didn't want to get caught between us. I appreciated that she and Paul hadn't so far "sided" with Claire and dumped me in the process. One dumping a year is enough.

"Lynn," Beth said firmly, "you know I don't like to be put in the middle of this."

"I tried to call her to talk," I said, cleverly omitting the fact that I been phone-harassing Claire for weeks, "but she's changed her number. It's unlisted."

"She was getting creepy calls late at night. A lot of hang-ups every evening around 11 o'clock. Then someone rang her buzzer at 3 in the morning. She got pretty freaked-out. Even reported it to the Gay and Lesbian Anti-Violence Project."

Jesus, I thought, *I'm contributing to the already high antigay violence statistics.* But at least the middle-of-the-night door buzzing wasn't my doing. Somehow that seemed worse than the hang-ups, much more threatening.

"Could you give me her new number?" I asked after a long pause.

Beth took a deep breath. "I'll ask her," she said finally.

Even though I was indeed a culprit, I felt morally outraged that Beth and Claire both suspected me. "You think *I* did it?"

"Let's just say people do all sorts of things when they've been hurt badly," Beth said diplomatically. "I'll tell Claire you want to talk to her, but that's the best I can do. Really."

Paul came back with a Diet Coke. "No ginger ale," he said. "I tried two stores. Maybe people don't drink it anymore. Come to think of it, I don't know the last time I drank a ginger ale."

The soda calmed my swaying stomach, and I started to feel like I would actually be able to move from the steps before the show let out and I was trampled to death. As we were all getting up to walk back to Beth and Paul's apartment, the door of the theater creaked open and a striking woman about Lexy's age with spiky black hair and a lobeful of earrings poked her head out. I remembered her as the ticket taker when we went into the performance.

"Hey, you okay?" she asked with concern.

"Yeah, I'm okay now," I explained, suddenly flushed with embarrassment that I hadn't been cool enough to stay for the whole show and anxious to find a good excuse. "I...I have mild asthma, and the stuffiness got to me."

Beth shot me a look of open-mouth surprise that I shrewdly ignored.

"Yeah, we definitely have a ventilation problem, but, hey, we're finally getting air-conditioning installed next week after this show's over," the young woman said. "Just in time for summer. So...come back again, okay?"

I promised that we would and flashed her my most engaging I'm-a-really-cool-forty-year-old-honest-I-am smile. Her raven head disappeared behind the door.

"I didn't know you had asthma," Paul said ingenuously.

"Neither did I." Beth cocked an eyebrow. "And I've known her thirteen years. You know, I'm willing to bet that right up until the moment she said it, Lynn didn't either." She turned to me with a self-righteous smirk. "Anybody want to place bets? Come on, five bucks."

"Fuck you," I said.

I've been lucky enough to make my living as a writer for the last twelve or so years, sort of an amazing feat, though it's not the kind of writing I'd most like to do. Ideally, I want to write plays, like I used to when I was a kid and aspiring to be a modern-day Jo March. I was the oldest and made my brother, Will, and baby sister, Amy (just like *Little Women!*), act in the plays with me along with our dog, Larry. Moe and Curly, the cats, wouldn't have any of it, but Larry always wanted to be wherever we were, right underfoot, a real dog's dog.

The only play I remember us performing was *Killer O'Connor*, in which Amy and I were newspaper reporters on the trail of a desperate murderer named O'Connor, played by Will. My brother was especially good at anything that required him to act psychotic. Amy was too little to really get it, so she just tagged along after me and did what I did. Larry was the police dog that went after the killer's scent. We charged a quarter admission and invited everyone in the neighborhood, and I think about ten kids came. I've never lost the taste for applause that play gave me.

My writing now is pretty tame compared to what I wrote in those days. My official title is "ghostwriter," and I've made a good living at it, specializing in working with people of "conscience" who want to write about the environment, for example, or the peace movement or popular feminism or animal rights. You know the best-seller *Greenhouse Rock*? Everyone thinks that F. Martin Martinson wrote that, but the truth is that I did. And April Ronsard, glamour feminist? Never wrote a word in her life. *Skin Deep* went from my computer to your bookshelf.

Which is all fine. Like I said, I've made a good living, and I haven't had to take assignments like ghostwriting the memoirs of, say, the person who sat across from Nicole Brown Simpson in kindergarten. But the sad truth is, my name has never appeared publicly on any piece of writing since I handprinted "a drama in three acts, by L.J. Woods" on the playbill of *Killer O'Connor* when I was twelve. I get effusive thanks in the acknowledgments of books — things like "For her invaluable help, support, and enthusiasm for this project..." and "I never could have done this without...." It's something, but it's never been quite enough.

When Claire and I were together, she encouraged me to stop ghostwriting and concentrate on something of my own. "Let me support us for a while," she generously offered. She had a good job as art director of a medium-size publishing house that specialized in lavishly illustrated coffee-table books.

"We can't cut our income in half just like that," I argued. "We're practically middle-aged."

"Oh, we are not. You're just afraid, and I understand that," Claire said. "But be honest about what scares you. Is it really the cut in income, or is it putting your own name on something for fear somebody will criticize you?"

Claire liked to cut to the root of a problem with one firm slash. It came from years of being successful in her job. On occasion, when I visited her office, I heard her talk to designers when she critiqued their work: "I like the general layout, but Goudy Old Style is wrong for this book. Pick another typeface" or "You've cropped too much of the action out of this photo. Try again." It was this same style of addressing a problem head-on that she used when we were standing at the corner of Astor Place and Lafayette, breaking up. Too bad *I* didn't get a chance to "try again."

In Claire's eyes, would I have been "enlarging myself" if I'd taken her up on her offer to support me while I wrote the next *Streetcar Named Desire* or *Angels in America*? It's hard not to wonder. She made some vague reference when she was leaving that made me think as much. She said, "It's time to stop being afraid," and when I asked of what, she merely replied, "Of life."

"Oh," I said. I still wasn't sure what she meant, but I pretended that she had cleared up my confusion. At the time, I thought she was talking about herself being afraid. But now I'm pretty sure she meant me.

So, believing that I was somehow taking her advice, I went back to P.J.'s.

"You're back!" Lexy said, putting a frosty Heineken down in front of me. "Did you, like, go away or something? It's been, I don't know, weeks."

It was hard to believe, after she rebuffed my offer of a drink two weeks before, that Lexy had noticed my absence from P.J.'s. She looked different: She had her hair tucked under a baseball cap (turned backward, of course) and was wearing an old LESBIAN AVENGERS — WE RECRUIT T-shirt with the sleeves cut off and the crew neckline scissored to a daring plunge. Her nose ring was now a diamond stud.

"I didn't know you were a Lesbian Avenger," I remarked, my eyes focused on the ignited bomb of the Avengers logo.

"I'm not," she said. "Never was. I just like the T-shirt." She was so completely guileless, it impressed me. In her position I probably would have made up anything to look good, like, "Yeah, I used to go to some of their actions."

"So where've you been?" she pursued, sitting down next to me. It was just before 10 o'clock, and P.J.'s hadn't filled up yet.

"Oh, I went to see Taylor Paris last week at Idiosyncrasy."

"He's transgendered, right? Or is it transsexual? I get confused." She put an elbow up on an empty chair, and I noticed for the first time that she had a tiny rose tattoo on the muscular underside of her upper arm. I'd already seen the small bunch of roses tattooed over her left breast, and it was like one had jumped from the bouquet right onto her arm.

"He's transsexual. He had what's called a sex reassignment."

"He became a woman?"

"No, he *was* a woman, a lesbian, who's now a man."

"That's intense."

"And his girlfriend is a lesbian who doesn't want to be with him now that he's a man."

"Wow." I thought she was getting bored, because she started looking around the room. Then, unexpectedly, she rested a Doc Martens boot on the rung of my chair. "Say, remember when you asked me to have a drink a couple of weeks ago?"

Uh-oh, I thought, here it comes. *This is when she tells me off thoroughly and completely. This is where I find out what a repulsive predator I really am.*

"Look, I'm sorry if you got the wrong idea…," I started.

19

She stared at me quizzically. "Oh, well, I just…well, okay then. Okay." She took a couple of short breaths and regrouped. "Well, maybe you won't want to then, but I was just going to ask if we could, like, get something to *eat* sometime, you know, instead of a drink? Since I don't drink? Some night after I get off?" She got off at 2 o'clock in the morning.

It was my turn to stare. She hadn't brushed me off at all. In my paranoia and her youth, we had just completely crossed our signals, mixed our messages, jammed our radar.

"How about tomorrow?" I suggested, settling back with my Heineken.

The next afternoon Harold helped me plan what he called my "date clothes." He really got into it, living vicariously through my experience. Harold hadn't had a date in over five years, since his boyfriend Mark left him and then a year later died of AIDS. Most of the problem was the agony of that experience for him, but part of it was also his own internalized homophobia — after living twenty years as exclusively gay, Harold still wasn't out to his parents. We'd had long, frustrating talks about how he needed to get back out on the front lines of dating, and occasionally he worked up the courage to ask friends to set him up with someone. I myself arranged a blind date for him with a researcher who had helped on one of the environmental books I'd written, a sweet young thing named Dennis whose favorite word was "glorious." But at the last minute, Harold had called to say he had a sore throat and couldn't possibly leave his apartment, maybe for several weeks. Would I please call Dennis and give his apologies? he croaked pathetically into the phone. After bailing him out, I refused to get involved again in his nonexistent love life.

"Lexy's a babe," Harold said approvingly, leaning back on my bed and watching me dig items of clothing out of my drawers and toss them onto the bedspread. "But I never took you for a chicken hawk, hon."

"I hate that term," I snapped, holding a blue vest up against a button-down striped shirt, then rejecting both of them. "It makes me sound like a pedophile."

"You could start a new trend in the lesbian community — woman-girl love. Wait, she has to be over twenty-one to be a waitress, right?"

"She's twenty-*three,* to be exact," I said sharply, as if there were a universe of difference between twenty-three and twenty-one. "How about this?" I held a burgundy vest, identical to the blue one, against a pink button-down shirt.

"Do you, uh, have anything besides vests and, uh, oxford-cloth shirts?" he asked cautiously.

"Too butch?" I asked.

"No, I was thinking too preppy. I mean, this girl has *tattoos,* hon." He fingered the burgundy vest but set it politely aside.

I sat down on the bed in my bra and underpants and stared down hopelessly at myself. Even my underwear, I knew, was wrong. Where was my athletic bra, my Calvin Klein shorts? Once at Macy's I tried on an athletic bra but had so much trouble taking it off, I almost had to cut myself out of it with my Swiss Army knife.

"It's hopeless," I moaned. "I don't have the right clothes to date a 23-year-old. I should run out and buy something new before tonight."

"Listen," Harold reasoned, giving the blue vest another inspection, "if she wanted someone who looked just like her, she wouldn't have agreed to the date. Why not just wear your regular clothes and be yourself? That's who she's interested in, isn't it?"

It seemed like good advice, but I still didn't like the look of the woman who put on the striped shirt and blue vest with uniformly faded Gap blue jeans. She had the appearance of someone stuck in 1980, when she was new to New York and her clothes were in fashion. My hair, a short, uncomplicated brown bob, hadn't changed much since then either.

At the last minute Harold suggested ripping a hole in the left knee of my jeans where the denim was beginning to wear thin. It wasn't quite right, but it was better than nothing. He also coaxed me into mismatched earrings, one post and one dangling. "I look ridiculous," I said. "I'm old."

"No, never," he disagreed, kneeling to tear the hole in my jeans a little bigger, until it seemed like the bottom half of my pant leg was going to come off. "You're a classic."

I expected Lexy to fall somewhere in the range between flaky and obtuse — admittedly, a narrow-minded stereotype of a Generation X girl. I hadn't talked to her much, only between beers at P.J.'s, so I knew very little about her. And I have to say that when she told me that Ethan Hawke was one of her favorite actors, that's when the stereotype started to form.

I don't like to confess all this, because it makes me look foolish and, well, predatory, like I was just in it for the sex. I hated feeling like a middle-age man, ogling and drooling over pretty young things. Let's say my judgment was impaired. Let's say that having a gorgeous young woman with tattoos and a pierced nose pay me any attention at all, let alone go on a *date* with me, gave my self-esteem a boost. Let's say that I thought, being a lesbian, that I was somehow above all that middle-aged male crap, that what I was doing was okay because I was a woman.

All right — as long as I'm admitting all this, I'll just go right ahead and say that, yes, I thought it would be one or two nights at most of rip-roaring sex.

I met Lexy late at P.J.'s, even though I didn't have anything to do before our 2 A.M. date but take a nap. I wanted to seem busy, active, tireless — P.J.'s and a date with Lexy was just a quick stop on my social calendar. By 2:15 we were on our way to an all-night diner just down the block, a place I'd never been to, though I'd passed it a million or so times in the fifteen years I'd lived in the neighborhood. It seemed too seedy to me, mostly because it didn't even have a name. Lexy called it Mac's, but where she got that from, I still don't know. There was no name over the door, no neon sign in the window except one for Budweiser, no headline on the comprehensive plastic-coated menus with their typewritten fare. "Want to go to Mac's?" she asked, as if everyone knew exactly what Mac's was.

"Sure," I replied, almost walking right by the diner. I was convinced Mac's had to be some trendy new spot in the East Village that we would walk to. Lexy had stopped a few paces behind me and stood looking at me curiously, one hand on the diner's front door.

"This is it," she said, holding the door open for me like any thoughtful escort might, and I tried to cover up the fact that I hadn't the slightest idea where or what Mac's was.

"I guess I'm in a daze," I laughed. "I'd probably walk right by my own apartment tonight!"

That was a lucky move, a quick recovery, since Lexy's rich smile told me she thought I was in a daze over her. Which I sort of was.

She was wearing the black leather vest she'd worn the first night at P.J.'s, which showed off her over-the-breast tattoo to perfection. When she breathed, the roses were instantly in bloom.

We sat at a corner booth that had sticky substances dotted all over it. Lexy's coffee mug stuck to one of them almost every time she put it down, but she didn't seem to care.

"You can drink caffeine this late at night?" I asked in wonder. Then I bit my lip. One sure way to mark yourself as old is to worry about drinking real coffee after dinner.

"I'm used to it, working so late," she said. "Besides, I can't stand most decaf. It just tastes like colored water to me."

I pushed my mug of decaf to the side of the table and picked at my small Greek salad instead. Lexy launched into a huge mound of french-fried onion rings, which she doused with salt, pepper, and ketchup. "Want some?" she offered. "There's nothing like Mac's onion rings."

I shook my head politely, watching in wonder as she ate every last one. Just looking at them was enough to give me indigestion, but the greasy, tantalizing smell drove me wild with desire. *Lynn, Lynn, Lynn,* I thought, *remember the days when you could eat like that at 2:30 in the morning, then have a milk shake to wash it all down?* My ability to eat anything fried and not gain ten pounds ended when I was thirty-six. It was so sudden, I never saw it coming. One day my metabolism just decided that she and I were getting too old for anything but salads, baked potatoes with a dash of pepper, and broiled fish.

Luckily I refrained from mentioning any of these thoughts out loud to Lexy. *Not the time,* I thought, *to call attention to my age.* Maybe she wouldn't notice that whole network of lines at the corners of my eyes or the thin, subtle streaks of gray in my hair that my hairdresser, Kyra, has been begging me for years to cover. "You'll look ten years younger!" she assures me.

The truth is, I believe that as we age, our bodies get older and we get smarter emotionally, if we're lucky, but we're always about the same age in our minds. It's a different age for everyone, depending on when we were happiest. For me it's hard to remember that I'm not twenty-two. That was the year I discovered sex with women, in a way that made me smack my head and say "Duh!" — the sudden lightbulb of realization about why things hadn't been working out with men clicking on. "Geez, you're a lesbian!" I said to myself. Now when someone asks how old I am, I have to stop myself every time from saying, "Twenty-two." It's not that I'd like to be that age again; it's just that, mentally, I never really left it.

So why, if I felt twenty-two, was it so hard to talk to Lexy, who was twenty-three? Maybe because when I was twenty-two, Jimmy Carter was president. Instead of giving me the upper hand, Lexy's youth made me tongue-tied. But she didn't seem to mind doing most of the talking. I inserted questions here and there, a "Right" or a "No kidding" when they seemed appropriate. Mostly she talked about a film she was entering in the Lesbian and Gay Experimental Film Festival, which wasn't really a film per se but a series of still photographs that she'd videotaped with a friend's borrowed camcorder. She didn't own one.

"Oh, I do," I said suddenly. "One of those little palm-corder things. Very cute."

"Yeah?" she said, suddenly animated. "You make movies too? You didn't tell me!"

"No, no, I don't. It was a present," I said, remembering suddenly that this was a bad direction to take. Harold had warned me to steer away from talking about Claire, and it was Claire who had given me the palm-corder on my fortieth birthday. I'd never even used it except that night, filming our friends stuffing chocolate mud cake into their mouths and popping the cork off the Moët & Chandon bottle. "From a friend."

"Nice friend!" Lexy said, impressed.

"Actually, an ex," I added and tried desperately to think of some way to change the subject before Lexy had a chance to zero in on it.

"Nice ex," she said. Then with a bored sigh, "All I got from my ex was a $300 phone bill."

What luck, I thought — *she's turned things around to herself again.* "Three hundred bucks! Why?"

"She, Moira, my ex, was making late-night calls to her ex, who's, like, trying to break into movies in California," Lexy said with a frown. "Moira would wait till I went to work, then stay on the phone for hours. Turns out they weren't so 'ex.' Doesn't that bite?"

"How did you end up with the bill?" I asked.

"The phone was in my name, and she split," Lexy explained. She looked uncomfortable, and I wondered if some thoughtful friend had advised her away from the subject of ex-lovers too. "The phone company was actually pretty nice about it. They're letting me pay it off thirty bucks a month. But a camcorder doesn't seem to be in my immediate future."

"Look," I said, feeling sympathy for her as a rejected lover, "you can borrow mine anytime."

"Your what?" she asked, looking over the menu again for something sweet.

"Camcorder."

"Really?" She signaled to the waitress and ordered a slice of chocolate cream pie.

"Sure, I never use it. Someone should." I wasn't certain I should dare it at that point — but if the main reason for the evening was sex, why not? "Want to stop in at my place and look at it? It's right around the corner."

"Wow, that's cool!" she said. "Really? You mean it?"

I did mean it. I meant it so much, my stomach flip-flopped and my armpits started to sweat.

I don't think of my apartment as anything much. It's a small walk-up off Third Avenue in the East Twenties that I've held the lease on since 1981, when you could still get a great deal on an apartment in this part of town. It wasn't where people new to the city, including me, wanted to live. And outsiders still tend to think of New York as the Village or SoHo or the Upper West Side, with nothing in between.

My neighborhood doesn't even seem to have a name. It's too poor to be Gramercy Park and too far south to be Murray Hill or Turtle Bay. Sometime in the late 1980s, a lot of gay people started showing up on the streets and in coffee shops and video stores. Last June my block held its first-ever Gay Pride party. So even though it doesn't have the charm of the Village, I really wouldn't consider living anywhere else.

I inherited the apartment from a college friend of mine, Andrea, who got married and moved to New Jersey with her husband, Sam. She wanted to hold on to the apartment as a pied-à-terre, but her husband (the quintessential "Suit") thought it meant she didn't trust that the marriage was going to last. So after subletting to me for six months, Andrea decided to turn the lease over, and I got a small but comfortable and affordable place. I've never seen her house in New Jersey, but I heard it has a heated pool and a tennis court.

When Claire and I got together, she wanted to find a bigger apartment, since one half of my living room was occupied by my desk, bookshelves, file cabinets, and other home office equipment. We looked around, but nothing was as good a deal as my little place. So we compromised. She moved in with me, and I rented cheap office space on East Twenty-third Street — actually, a partitioned-off desk and bookshelf in the office of a now-defunct leftie newspaper, *Pinko Rag*. That's where I met Harold, who used to keep their books for them and for an array of other fringe organizations.

Anyway, the point is that my apartment is no showplace. I have a dark blue pullout sofa from Jennifer Convertibles with a couple of rips in the fabric, and a sleek Danish chair from IKEA. There's an antique oak chair that Claire and I found abandoned on the street and refinished. The floorboards aren't in such great shape, so I've covered them with room-sized cotton area rugs. All the floors slant slightly toward the south. I've never owned a real stereo system, just a boom box, and my TV was new when you could ride the subway for under a dollar. There's a glass coffee table that Claire and I bought each other one Christmas. Bookshelves are everywhere, in the living room, lining the hallway, in the bathroom, in the bedroom. A few years back I decided I was too old to have posters thumbtacked to the walls the way I always had, and I splurged on cheap frames for everything. If I had to choose a phrase to describe the place, it would be simply "lived-in."

So I was surprised when Lexy enthused, "What a cool apartment!" Another Generation X stereotype shot to hell — maybe they didn't all aspire to designer apartments?

"Yeah?" I said, taking a seat on the sofa. Claire always said the midnight blue brought out the color of my eyes. "You think so?"

"Yeah, I really do."

"Oh, it's not such a big deal," I said modestly, trying to picture the place from her perspective.

"It is if you've seen *my* place," she laughed. "It's, like, 'Early vegetable crate.' "

"Well, I'm a lot older...." Shit, there it was, out in the open. I heard Harold's voice as a little murmur in my ear: *If you don't want to talk about the age difference, just don't bring it up.*

"Oh, you're not that much older," Lexy said, fingering a picture on the mantle of Claire and Harold at Lewes Beach, Delaware. It had been an unusually cold day in late August, and they were huddled together against the wind with powerful waves cresting behind them. Claire looked so happy and beautiful. It was a tormenting picture that I kept around just so I could feel sorry for myself. "What are you, maybe thirty?"

My palms moistened, and my tongue went dry. "Flattery will get you everywhere," I said, trying to turn an uncomfortable conversation into a flirtation.

It seemed to work. She tossed her head with a laugh, coppery waves falling forward over her eyes. "It will, huh?" she said, and I thought I'd successfully pushed her away from age and onto the sex track. She tucked herself up next to me on the couch and ran her fingers lightly through my hair — a gesture sure to drive a woman wild. "So, come on, Lynn...how old *are* you?"

This girl was no twinkie. She wasn't about to be lured away from the topic at hand by the mere promise of getting laid.

"Lexy...," I said, squirming.

"Thirty-three?"

"Lexy, come on...."

"Thirty-five!"

It was too painful, so I had to stop her. "I'm forty, okay?" I realized that it had come out blunt and sharp, not at all the way I'd intended on an evening when I was hoping to score.

"Wow!" she said, pulling back a little, probably because I sounded so incensed. "You're kidding."

"Would I kid?" I said, trying to soften my tone. After my maternal sharpness, sex was probably out of the question now.

"Yeah, you crack jokes all the time," Lexy said. "That's one of the things I really like about you, your sense of humor. You're really funny, you know?"

"Well, when you get to be my age, it's no laughing matter," I said, laughing.

"Wow, forty," she said, letting it sink in. I scanned her face, trying to imagine what she was thinking: *My mother's forty-something. This woman could be my mother — well, almost. She's another generation — what are we going to talk about?*

Deciding to take matters into my own hands and rescue a bad situation from getting worse, I jumped off the couch and plucked my camcorder off the shelf where it had been sitting for the longest time collecting dust. I blew the excess off and brought it over to her for inspection with a strained, I'm-not-really-changing-the-subject smile on my face. "I almost forgot why we came here!" I said, holding out the camera shyly.

She glanced at me, puzzled, and then at the camcorder, which I had shoved into her hands. "I guess I'm, like, dense or something," she said, putting it down on the coffee table. She reached up and yanked me toward her by my belt buckle. "I thought we came here to fuck."

That was the first date with Lexy.

The rest is sort of a velvety blur, all naked breasts and thighs and butts in the air. I do remember, though, that it was the first time I ever had to consider safer sex. Claire and I were together pre-AIDS, or at least pre-safer sex, and amazing as it seems to Harold and other gay male friends, we were monogamous the entire time.

"Not even one little transgression?" Harold asked after the breakup. "Not one casual buddy-fuck somewhere along the way?"

"We *lived* together, Harold," I pointed out, as if that somehow ensured fidelity. "And most of *my* buddies have been gay men."

For me safer sex was a new frontier. I didn't have anything in my apartment that even vaguely resembled a condom or a dental dam except a roll of generic plastic wrap. Lexy, who had never had sex *without* first thinking about AIDS, searched the kitchen cabinets in vain for something more durable and brand-name.

"Forget it," I said. "I don't buy regular Saran Wrap. Too expensive."

"Well," she said cheerfully, starting to rip off a sheet of flimsy plastic, "I guess this will have to do!"

"You don't have to use it on me," I said, shyly helpful. "Thirteen years with the same woman. And I haven't had sex with a man since 1975."

The "thirteen years" must have given her pause, but it was the "1975" that really stopped her. "Nineteen seventy-*five*?" she said, her emphasis making it sound like 40 B.C. "Wow!"

She handed the plastic sheet to me. "I don't have your record," she smiled. "I've had to think about safer sex forever. And," she added slowly, "I had this good friend from college who was bi, and he and I used to, you know, fuck sometimes when we were both lonely and couldn't get a date. Always with condoms, though."

It was hard to believe that this stunning young woman ever had trouble getting a date. I blushed the color of the crimson roses on her breast as I took the thin plastic wrap, which was already sticking to itself. I followed her into the bedroom, trying to untangle it and thinking, *This will be a challenge.*

I can't really describe the terror of sleeping with someone new after thirteen years of marriage — and thirteen years in which the last five years of sex went something like this:

[*Kiss, kiss*] You feel like it tonight?

[*Kiss, kiss*] Sort of, but I'm so tired. [*Yawn*]

Me, too. [*Yawn*] How about next Saturday?

It's a date. [*Snore*]

[*Snore*]

I wasn't even quite sure what I was supposed to do with the plastic wrap. Should I just casually spread it over her like she was a deli sandwich? Somewhere in the middle of it all, I remember, the plastic fogged up and moistened with the "dew of love." I couldn't see or feel anything, and I was concentrating so much on holding the damn dam in place that I wasn't doing a very thorough or accurate job. To my great embarrassment, Lexy stopped me midlick.

"Fuck me," she said hoarsely. Claire had never said that in my memory. Our sex life had been stuck somewhere in the early 1980s, when the standard lesbian directive, even at the pinnacle of passion, was "Use your fingers."

I gulped, and then I tossed the soggy sandwich wrap over the side of the bed and into the trash can. Two points!

"There'll be no *living* with you now," Harold said mischievously when we met for dinner the next night. "You're like the cat that swallowed the canary. Oops, I mean the chicken. Yum."

"Will you stop with the age jokes?" I said, annoyed. "They're getting old, Harold."

" 'Old' age jokes — very funny," he laughed. "Come on — the details."

Feeling my whole face heat up, I dove into my menu.

"Your ears just turned red!" Harold squealed. "I never saw your *ears* turn red!"

"Look, I'm not used to talking about sexual exploits, okay?" I said in a whisper.

"You never had any to talk about," he pointed out, taking the liberty of ordering two glasses of wine. "You're definitely going to be more fun now!"

"Oh, Harold."

He must have realized he'd gone too far, that Claire was still considerably more than a faded memory. "Oh, Lynn." He ordered a pasta dish, and even though I wanted grilled chicken, I ordered salmon instead. I couldn't take anymore of Harold's puns.

"Okay, I'll tell you this much — it was fun. It was definitely fun. Unusual but fun. And very, very casual," I concluded.

"What makes you think so?" he asked with a cocked eyebrow.

"Because I don't want to spend all my time with someone who was four years old when I was graduating from college," I noted. I wasn't sure my arithmetic was right, and I could see Harold, the tax man, doing the calculations in his head. "It was exciting, sure, but—"

"But what? Look, you just got divorced. You don't have to be looking for another spouse right away. Live a little." It was funny advice coming from someone who never dated, but his own situation was so complicated, I couldn't even broach the topic anymore.

"Well, after the incident with the sandwich wrap, I—"

"*What?* Come on, Lynn, don't be cruel — I want details!"

"Never mind," I said, purposely toying with him. "It's just that I don't know how anxious she'll be to jump in the sack with a mom-figure again. Can we switch topics?" I asked as our entrées arrived.

He sipped his wine and looked at me cautiously over his glass. "Well, come to think of it, I have an eensy-weensy favor to ask."

"No, I won't cat-sit for Endora again," I said firmly. His inky black cat, named for Samantha's mother on *Bewitched,* was well-named. The last time I checked in on her when Harold was out of town on business, she sat sizing me up from across the room for an hour or so, and then, when I was leaning over to change the water in her dish, she lunged at me and put a few well-placed claw marks in my neck. "That cat's possessed by the spirit of Agnes Moorehead."

"She was just mad at me for going away," he said defensively. "But that's not the favor anyway."

I waited, spearing a healthy piece of fish. He wound some angel hair with pesto around his fork and bit his lip.

"Oh, no," I said, shaking my head with the sudden realization of what the favor was. "Not that again!"

"Come on, it's been a whole year since I asked you to go with me," he whined.

"No, Harold," I said firmly. "I told you last time that I would never go to visit your family again."

Harold, who wasn't out to his family, had, on a couple of occasions, charmed me into accompanying him as his beard to big family shindigs in Westchester. I'd been to his parents' fortieth anniversary and his sister Janet's wedding, two celebrations of heterosexuality that I could have done without. At both I'd been repeatedly interrogated by Harold's mother and aunt about whether I would consider converting to Judaism when Harold and I finally tied the knot.

"Come on, it wasn't so bad, was it? Besides, it's Bubbe's ninetieth birthday, and you *love* Bubbe." I could tell that pouting was going to be the next phase.

"Look, Harold, I don't want to give up my Sunday to go all the way up to Chappaqua with you," I said. "I've got a lot to do."

It was true, though — I did love Harold's grandmother. She was a classic, snow-haired and tiny, with a thick Yiddish accent. When Harold introduced me to her at his parents' anniversary party, Bubbe sat me down in a corner, took my hands, and stared earnestly into my face. "So," she said, invoking a solemn tone that suggested this was my test as a future granddaughter-in-law, "vhere do you buy your chickens?"

"I promise, this is the last time," Harold pleaded. "It's three weeks from today. I'm going to tell them I'm gay, and I need all the support I can get."

"You're going to come out at Bubbe's birthday party?" I asked in horror. I could see it — the room crammed with relatives, the cake being wheeled out ablaze with candles, Bubbe standing to blow them out, and then…Harold dropping the bomb. The Fines were a dramatic brood, right on down to Harold, and I envisioned a lot of head slapping and chest thumping as the family absorbed the latest shock.

"Not at the actual party," he snapped impatiently. "But yeah, sometime that day. My therapist agreed it might be best to tell them right before I leave so they can mull over it alone." He hadn't taken a bite of his pesto, though he was looking at it wistfully. I kept at my salmon silently and resolutely.

"I'm renting a car this time," he pointed out. "We wouldn't have to schlepp on the train. And we could leave anytime we want…."

I sipped my chardonnay.

"Please? Bubbe loves you too. Won't you come — for Bubbe?"

"Oh, yeah," I said sarcastically, "Bubbe's gonna *love* me after this trip."

For days after my date with Lexy, all I could think about was sex. I hadn't had any in roughly six months, and the all-night-right-through-till-dawn session with her had opened doors of possibilities for me. At noon, when she left my apartment, we were cool and noncommittal. "Let's talk soon," she said, planting a wet kiss on my lips, and I casually agreed, "Yeah, let's." Within days I wasn't limiting Lexy to a one- or two-night fling. Suddenly we would be regular fuck buddies, to use Harold's term, with no strings attached.

In lust, not love, I was determined not to call Lexy too soon, to wait a few days and make a date for the weekend. Besides, my forty-year-old body couldn't really take an all-nighter in the middle of the week. After Saturday I'd slept in for two days straight and then wandered around like a New York neophyte. One night of sex had wrapped a soft blanket of fog around me that made it harder to function in the quick, hard world of the city that I was so accustomed to.

Images of me and Lexy in all sorts of sexual positions came to me at the most awkward and unlikely times. In the checkout line at Food Emporium, I dropped a liter bottle of seltzer on the big toe of the woman behind me in line because I wasn't paying attention. "It's probably broken!" she bellowed. But then she calmed down when the pain subsided and stopped mumbling about lawsuits. At the ATM at the bank, I became mesmerized by the screen and accidentally pushed the button to read the transactions in Chinese instead of English. It took an extra thirty seconds to exit and start over in English, and the man who was next on line murmured his discontent to the person behind him: "If they don't know how to *use* the damn machines, why don't they go to a teller?"

But before I had a chance to call her, Lexy was on the line to me, though I didn't remember giving her the phone number. "Surprise!" she said. "It was hard to find you. 'L. Woods' is a pretty common name. There had to be, like, fifteen in Manhattan, and none on East 24th Street."

"I get my mail at a P.O. box," I said. "For business purposes." That sounded like a convincing reason, but I really did it because I didn't like having my address right there in the NYNEX white pages for everyone to see. Being a phone stalker myself, I knew all too well how something as common as a telephone line could be used as an assault weapon.

"Well, I tried three numbers before I finally got you," she said, a touch of annoyance in her voice. "If this hadn't been you, I'd have been camping out on your street!"

37

That should have told me something about Lexy's feelings toward me, but it didn't. Or maybe I just didn't want to think about having a 23-year-old infatuated with me and being a potential stalker herself. All I wanted to think about were the sex toys she claimed to have a whole collection of: "I hid them so Moira wouldn't get them." That's what I like, a girl with definite priorities. She might have a $300 phone bill dumped on her, but at least she still had her dildos and butt plugs.

"I was just going to call you," I said to steer us onto less-complicated terrain. "You busy Friday after work?"

"N-o-o-o," she said, slowly. "But I was hoping to see you sooner. Like tonight."

"Tonight?" Tonight was only Tuesday. This wasn't the way it was supposed to go. We were supposed to get a week off between dates so that the sex would stay fresh and exciting for as long as possible. I thought as quickly as I could, even though a wave of desire coursed through me. "Oh, I can't tonight. Dinner with a friend."

"How about we meet late, after dinner?" she persisted.

"No, we'll probably go to a movie too. I don't know when I'll get home." It was only a partial lie. Dinner was upstairs with my neighbors Jonathan and Alec, the ones with the rainbow flag. When they invited me over (which seemed to be a lot since Claire left), they always sent me home by ten so Alec, who had AIDS, wouldn't get too worn out. "I don't like to be that kind of friend," I said. "You know, 'Sorry, but I gotta go get laid now.' "

She laughed, as I had hoped she would. "No, that'd be rude."

"Yeah, wouldn't it? So how about Friday?" I asked again, determined to try to turn things around to my timetable.

"Sure, sure, Friday after work is great. We'll pull another all-nighter." She lowered her voice, and I remembered that she had a roommate. "I'll bring my toys."

The thought of Lexy and her toys made me all creamy. Claire and I had gone to the sex store called the Pleasure Chest one Saturday, but we had been too shy to buy anything. In fact, we'd been too intimidated to stay for more than about three minutes. "Did you see all those hoods?" I asked, referring to a wall lined with leather masks and headgear for nights of S/M fun. Lexy's toys, she said, were from a women's store she had visited in San Francisco.

"I can't wait for you to *fuck* me," Lexy whispered with just the right amount of pressure on the word "fuck."

"Me too," I admitted, weakly. "Look, wait...let me call my friend and see if I can rearrange our dinner tonight."

"Yeah?" Lexy asked, her eagerness reminding me a little of my old dog, Larry, when he was a puppy.

"Yeah," I said, ashamed to yield so quickly to lascivious talk but doing it anyway. Then, even more butch, "Yeah."

I could have made up some story about being sick or overworked to tell Jonathan and Alec, but I didn't bother. They live right upstairs and could easily have seen me and Lexy together in the hallway. Or heard us through the air shaft. Getting caught in a lie by those two sweethearts would have torn me up.

"Look, I've been getting laid for the first time in six months," I explained to them, "and I've become kind of a sex addict. I'm serious. Next stop, Sexual Compulsives Anonymous."

"My dear," Jonathan replied with complete understanding, "say no more."

"Just promise you'll come back tomorrow," Alec called after me, "and tell us all about it!"

Lexy arrived at 8 with a sleek leather backpack that seemed too expensive for someone on her salary. I stroked it appreciatively.

"Nice bag," I commented, kissing her lightly on the lips.

"It's full of surprises," she purred.

It was after the Indian takeout that we barely touched, just as Lexy was opening up her bag of tricks and laying the contents out in a tantalizing row across the living-room rug, that I had a premonition. I knew that the phone was going to ring about ten seconds before it actually did. At a moment like that, with candles burning softly and Lexy displaying her toys like a shopkeeper of love, I should have let the machine pick up. But this, you may remember, was before I stopped answering the phone.

"Can't you let the machine get it?" Lexy said with the same puppylike pleading she'd used with me on the phone. I almost gave in to her, but then, I'd had the feeling that it was going to ring. What if it was a death in the family, an emergency upstairs with Alec?

Okay, maybe it was sexual-performance anxiety that made me run to answer it and not some high-minded concern about a relative or friend. The phone rang just as Lexy was pulling out a smooth black leather harness with lots of intimidating buckles and a thick, pink-colored dildo.

"I'll just be a minute, honest," I promised, rushing to the bedroom to get the call on the last ring before the machine clicked on.

"Hello?" I said, breathless.

There was a pause and then a painfully familiar voice. "Lynn? Did I, uh, interrupt something?"

"Claire!" I lowered my voice. "*Claire* — how are you?" I ignored her question, hoping to guide her away from it. Lying to Claire was not my strong suit. "Did Beth tell you I tried to call?"

"Yes," Claire said slowly. I could tell she was weighing the merits of pursuing the question about interrupting me, then quietly dropping the idea. "I've been good. Actually, much better now that the crank calls have stopped."

"Beth said someone rang your buzzer too. In the middle of the night."

"Yeah, but that just happened once. How are *you*?" She seemed stiff and proper, like someone I had met only a couple of times who didn't have much to say to me.

"I'm okay," I said. "I'm...I miss you." Why did I throw that in? And in such a faint, droopy whisper, because I was afraid that Lexy would hear me.

"Well, I...sometimes I miss you too," she admitted, but her tone was so distant that it was hard to believe she felt anything for me at all. "But, Lynn, I think we've got a problem."

Had we divided up the books wrong? Did she want the glass coffee table we'd bought together? Had she discovered that she was missing some underwear?

If only it had been one of those things.

"You know what I mean."

I did, but there was no way on earth that I could admit it. The magazine subscriptions were harmless enough, but phone harassers are scum, and badgering someone I had loved for thirteen years seemed to make me the lowest of the low. How did she know? How could she tell from a simple click of the receiver? Worse yet, how could she think I'd ring her buzzer after midnight, scaring her half to death? "Don't you? Don't you know exactly what I mean?"

"I'm not sure I do," I said to avoid the whole conversation. The reality hit me of Lexy sitting patiently on the floor in the other room while I had a heart-to-heart with Claire. "Look, Claire, do you want to get together and discuss what our 'problem' is? I can't really go into it right now. Someone's here."

Someone's here. I admit it, I said it to hurt her. I wanted her to think that, yes, she had caught me in the middle of strenuous sex. In fact, I wanted a detailed picture of it to keep flashing through her mind all night long.

You always hurt the one you love....

But Claire ignored the blow. "Lynn, I want to make an appointment for us in the next few weeks with the gay mediation service," she announced quickly without breathing. "Which nights are good for you?"

"Jesus, Claire, can't we just go for coffee or something?" I said. "Why are you dragging someone else into this...this whatever it is?"

"Because I'm tired of your games. Personally I think you need professional help. But I'm willing to try to talk to you, given that we had all those years together. And I want someone else to be there, because I think it's going to be hard on both of us."

It was too ridiculous and tiring to keep up the mask of righteous innocence, so I gave in. "Tuesdays," I allowed. "Tuesdays and Thursdays are generally good."

I could hear fast and furious scribbling on her end of the line. "Okay, then, I'll let you know when we get an appointment." I'm not sure who said good-bye first or if we even did. The next thing I knew, the receiver was out of my hand and resting on its cradle again.

Lexy had either gotten bored or tired of listening in and had switched the radio on to a rap station I'd never even known existed. The toys were all out of the bag, with the dildo in the middle of the floor, bobbing on end like a penis growing right out of the rug. She was sprawled next to them with only her T-shirt on, no jeans or underwear, filming them with the camcorder. "That the 'friend' you blew off tonight?" she asked cautiously from behind the camera.

"What? Oh, no, just somebody I'm not getting along with very well," I replied, carefully heeding Harold's advice about ex-lover talk. "Sorry it took so long. I see you've kept busy."

"Yeah — hey, sex is kind of like art, don't you think?" she asked, jumping up and turning the camcorder on me. I had never thought of sex being like art and couldn't come up with any connections between the two things at all, hard as I tried. A flash of embarrassment went through me for not being able to follow the analogy of a 23-year-old. I held a hand up to shield my face from the camera, but she just kept winding around me, filming my discomfort.

"Stop, *please,*" I begged.

"I bet you say that to all the girls," she grinned, tossing me the harness, which I failed to catch and which landed with a click of metal buckles at my feet. "Here, babe, let's see how you look in leather." Then she pitched the dildo at me, which I also missed, and it bounced playfully on the rug. I picked it up and, to break the tension of holding the thing, wagged it at her and said, "I'll get you, my pretty!"

I may have been making a joke, but after that night I appreciated penises a little more. There was something very powerful about strapping on Lexy's harness and dildo, especially when it was she who buckled the whole assembly into place. It sounds unlikely, but it was like I got this incredible hard-on. I suddenly wanted to take her everywhere but in the bed — against the door, on the rug, bent over a chair. I was the animal I never dreamed of being.

"You're *wild*" is the way Lexy put it when we finally stopped in the middle of the night, more from exhaustion than anything else. "You make my cunt ache."

I couldn't remember anyone ever telling me I made her cunt

ache, especially not Claire, and a flicker of something that was a mixture of both power and sadness lit up in me. If I had been alone, I might have let myself cry a little before falling asleep. But instead I wrapped Lexy against me with both arms and said in my best tough-girl manner, "There's more where that came from."

By now it probably seems to you that I only talk about working but don't actually do it. The truth is somewhere in between. While all this was starting up with Lexy, I was in the middle of the initial planning stages for April Ronsard's new book, tentatively titled *Pink and Blue*, about how there are real biological differences between women and men that shouldn't be ignored but that society should work with to reach equality for all. For example, if anthropological "evidence" indicates that women have evolved throughout time as nurturers and negotiators, maybe women are *naturally* suited to be politicians, lawyers, and diplomats.

It's a controversial subject and one I have some difficulty with. I can't help it; it feels like an antifeminist argument to me. I do believe that men and women have fundamental differences, but continually bringing up the question of "nature versus nurture" disturbs me. It's always been too easy for people in power to use arguments of biological difference to justify discrimination.

It also bothers me that April almost always avoids lesbians in her arguments, no matter how much I push her on the subject. With the first book, April and I had some heated discussions about it, but she contends that she's not homophobic, like some of the other big names in '90s feminism. "I've had more crushes on women in my life than I could even *tell* you about," she says in her defense.

Usually, I'm a conscientious worker with good discipline and follow-through. You have to be to do well in freelance writing. But when the affair with Lexy took off, my start-up work on the new book lagged. Against my better judgment, Lexy and I were spending a lot of nights together, and I was exhausted all the time, sleeping in until 1 or 2 in the afternoon some days. Which means I did no work for about two weeks, inadvertently skipped one meeting with April and was a day early for another, then finally realized that if I blew it and lost this job, Lady Lust wasn't going to pay my rent. Luckily, April was willing to cut me a lot of slack, because *Skin Deep* had been such an enormous best-seller. She needed my words as much as I needed the money.

I couldn't admit to April that my inertia on the project was due to a sudden voracious appetite for sex with a woman almost half my age, so I lied, took the high road, and said a good friend was ill and I was taking care of him. I didn't mention AIDS, but that's what people immediately think when a lesbian or gay man says a male friend is "ill," and they're usually correct. I *have* been there, just not at that time.

"Of course, of course," April said in her most I've-seen-*Angels in America* tone, and I felt a twinge of shame and remorse — almost like I'd betrayed Alec and my other friends who were ill — that made me decide to do penance for my vile lie.

So although Lexy whined like an unattended car alarm, I stayed home alone the night before the next scheduled meeting with April, knowing I couldn't afford to sleep through it. I went to bed at 10 o'clock and woke at dawn, feeling purified and ready to go.

46

I had my notes, I had my outline, I had my lesbian guard up. I even had my one pair of linen pants pressed. I always dressed a little better for my meetings with April so I wouldn't feel like a complete *shlump*. April had exquisite clothes, a lot of smooth silks and crisp linens that never seemed to wrinkle, no matter how much she crossed and uncrossed her shapely legs. She was far more attractive in person than on her author photos, in which she was always smiling seductively and throwing back her head of curly chestnut hair. At meetings she was more au naturel, wearing very little makeup on her luminous, peachy skin, pulling her glossy hair into a perfect French braid, and looking about fifteen years younger than her real age, which had to be somewhere around fifty. If she hadn't been so blatantly heterosexual, homophobic, insincere, *and* my employer, I might have been on her like flannel dykes on a potluck dinner.

I arrived at April's apartment at a minute to 10 — never too early, or she wasn't ready yet. She had a whole morning ritual that she once explained to me in exhaustive detail. It included everything from a yogurt and carrot-juice shake to twenty minutes of meditation to a five-mile run in Central Park, and she had it timed to the minute. Her afternoons were filled with personal appearances, talk-show tapings, fund-raising lunches (she was an active member of the boards of several nonprofit organizations), and general self-promotion. Whenever I wondered why she didn't actually write her books herself — she was certainly smart and articulate and perfectly capable of doing so — the only answer I could come up with was that, as a professional celebrity, she didn't have time.

When I pushed her door buzzer, something unexpected happened. Usually April answered the door herself. She had a grand old apartment on Central Park West that was about ten times the size of mine, and it often took her a full five minutes to get to the door, even though the doorman downstairs had told her I was on my way up. Dramatic effect, I guess, or else sheer self-absorption. This time the door opened just seconds after my finger hit the bell.

"Hi! You must be Lynn Woods."

A lovely creature, a young April clone, stood in the doorframe. Her dark blond hair was braided just like April's, and her clothes were a less expensive version of her boss's. I was guessing Smith or Barnard, class of '92 or '93.

"I'm Jude Mann, April's new assistant," she introduced herself, holding out a hand to me across the doorway. I expected her handshake to match April's, which was a little like a cooked lasagna noodle, but instead it was solid and confident and seemed to say, "I'm young, I'm bright, this is a great job for me, I'm on my way."

"Lynn Woods," I announced, realizing a minute too late that she'd already said my name for me. To cover my blunder, I butched up my handshake, and our hands stayed locked in place for a fraction of a second longer than hands usually do in an introduction. I'm not making this up — Jude held on to it for an extra second and smiled in a way that made my gaydar go off. *Jesus, Lynn,* I thought, *could you please find someone over thirty to flirt with?*

"Am I too early?" I asked just to ask something.

"No, April's dictating some letters for me. She'll be right with us."

Jude led me into the living room, where coffee and the familiar no-fat muffins were waiting. Personally, I'd rather just avoid muffins than pretend that the egg-white and fruit-juice ones could possibly taste like those made with oil, refined sugar, and whole eggs. April went to a lot of expense to avoid fat, but her healthful treats always looked and tasted like something even a dog might reject. I let Jude pour me some coffee into a flowered china cup.

"April didn't tell me she hired a new assistant," I said to make small talk. "What happened to Ross?" Ross was the last assistant, a 24-year-old Princeton grad who pretended to know something about everything even though much of what he spouted off was incorrect. I had found him intolerable, but then I have a low threshold of tolerance for young men, especially straight ones from Ivy League schools. My personal prejudices aside, there was something a little smarmy between Ross and April that made me think they were on *closer* terms, if you know what I mean. Now it looked as if she had tired of her boy toy.

"Ross got a job at *GQ*," Jude reported. "April helped him get it. She says he thought opening her mail and typing her letters were really beneath him. Now he's opening mail and typing letters for some *male* editor, so I guess that's less demeaning!"

We both laughed, already coconspirators. "And what about you?" I asked. "How'd you get this job?" It sounded like I meant that the job was a plum, but I was actually thinking how demanding it would be working in the same space with April. At least I got to write at home and have some breathing space.

"Oh, I graduated from Vassar a few years ago..." (Well, I was close, anyway.) "...and I traveled around for a while. The Far East mostly." I had traveled after college too — cross-country in a secondhand '68 Volkswagen Beetle, camping all the way to California. "Kind of aimless, I guess. Then my mother heard about this job — she was in a CR group with April years and years ago, and they've been on the board of NOW together. And, well, here I am."

"Who's your mother?" I wondered. I had become acquainted with many of April's women's movement colleagues and didn't remember one named "Mann."

"Jill Womann." Jude blushed with embarrassment at owning the mother who had made an early reputation carving oversized wooden sculptures of women's genitals. "She legally changed her name and mine from 'Mann' in 1972, when she and my father got divorced, but I got rid of 'Womann' the minute I hit eighteen and had some say in it. I mean, high school with a name like that was hard enough. Sometimes radical feminists just went too far, don't you think?"

I myself had never considered changing my name. I couldn't imagine introducing myself as Lynn Marthadaughter or Lynn Labiaflower with a straight face. But I understood how hard it would have been for Jude's mother in the early '70s to have the name Mann (her *husband's* name, no less!) and be taken seriously as a feminist artist. I wondered if Jill Womann regretted the moniker she'd given herself, now that she was working on more abstract, less specifically woman-identified pieces.

"Lynn, Lynn, Lynn." April floated in, raising a cloud of incredibly expensive perfume around her. "Lynn." She hugged me loosely, almost like she changed her mind mid hug.

"April."

"How *is* your friend?"

"Oh, uh, better, thanks," I stumbled.

She looked stricken with concern. "You know, my hairdresser, Gregory, is the most delightful gay man. I can't bear the thought of anything happening to him! I literally, *literally* would fall apart." She sat down and motioned to Jude for some coffee, her face suddenly clearing of worry. "So you met my new little goddess-send!"

"Yeah, it was a surprise," I said, accepting a refill of coffee. "I didn't know Ross had left."

"Well…," she sniffed, shaking her head, "all I can say is, he'll be *much* happier at *GQ*." I was dying to know what had caused their rift but wouldn't dream of asking. Maybe Jude knew more and would divulge it at another time. "It's so much *easier* working with women, so much less *complicated*. I know you're going to love Jude as much as I do, Lynn. She's a jewel, just a *jewel!*"

I glanced over at Jude, who was in fact looking sort of bright and gemlike. *Topaz,* I thought, *or amber — something clear and fiery.* I concentrated as hard as I could, but I couldn't have disagreed with April more — working with women, especially very pretty young ones, could sometimes be incredibly complicated.

I made note immediately of how often Jude called me up with questions and messages from April, because Ross had almost never bothered to ask or tell me anything. In fact, he usually answered April's questions himself, figuring, I suppose, that a Princeton BA in English was about equal to twelve years of professional writing experience. I often caught his mistakes later.

Claire had maintained that Ross was just plain scared of me and that I read too much into his lack of communication skills. "If *you* were a 24-year-old straight man, don't you think you'd have a few pre-conceived notions about lesbians?" she asked. "And, honey, you can be one scary lesbian."

Jude didn't share her predecessor's fear of me. I talked to her five or six times in the first few days after we'd met, always casually and easily — just like when I'd met Lexy but miraculously without the aid of beer. I know I said my gaydar went off with Jude, but as you get older and everyone around you is getting younger, you become less sure of your ability to instantaneously spot another lesbian. At least, that's been the case for me. When I came out the lesbians I knew all used to dress a certain way, but now the rules have changed. And if your gaydar's aged right along with you, well, you can run into some problems.

Believe me, I can spot the obvious dykes. The first time I saw k.d. lang on TV I literally ran into the bedroom to get Claire. "You've gotta see this. There's this big old *dyke* singing on TV!" I yelled excitedly. But the ones that blur the boundaries, like Jude, make me cautious of drawing any conclusions from frequent phone calls and a longer-than-average handshake.

I wasn't even convinced of her sexual orientation when Jude asked me out to lunch. "I have your contract for you," she gave as the excuse. "And your advance check. I also wanted to ask you some advice about the work you do. You know, writing professionally."

"You're interested in writing?"

"Well, it's the one thing I'm sort of even a little bit good at," she sighed, but I was certain she was underrating herself. Women so often do, especially young women. "Unfortunately, I didn't inherit my mother's artistic talent."

"Oh, I bet you're selling yourself short."

"No. Let me put it this way: The one time I tried to sculpt something, I almost severed an artery." She laughed nervously. "Then I tried safer things, like oils and watercolors, charcoal. Oh, and clay. Jill was *determined*. I broke her heart."

"I doubt it," I reassured her. "I'm sure she's very proud of you." *How foolish and insipid,* I thought right after I'd said it. Maybe Jill tormented her every day of her life about not being an artist. What did *I* know?

"Yeah, well, anyway…." Jude was very quiet and probably anxious by then to get off the phone. "So Thursday at 1, right?"

"Thursday at 1." Thursday afternoon was a good day for a mild flirtation with Jude. Wednesday night I was seeing Lexy, so I'd be feeling up for it, attractive and killer-sexy. And Thursday night I had to meet with Claire and a faceless lesbian mediator by the name of Jocelyn Truitt.

"I was wondering," Lexy mused as we munched on pretzels and an apple, the only things left in my house after a Sunday spent in bed, "why we never go out."

I sat up with a quick glance down at my stomach to make sure it wasn't sagging unattractively. I was always doing this around Lexy, furtively sucking in my gut, trying to hide unsightly flab, all because she was so willowy and flat-bellied. When I was twenty-three I was shaped very similarly, and people used to tease me that I had no hips or ass. I embodied a certain young lesbian aesthetic, more like a teenage boy than a woman.

Maintaining a passable body at forty took some work. I'd completely cut out sweets of any kind and was spending three hours a week at the city gym in my neighborhood. It's an old city-run bathhouse on East Twenty-third Street that's been converted into a public gym and costs only twenty-five dollars a year to join. For the convenience and the economy, you have to put up with a lot of big, sweaty men who seem to work out at all times of the day and night. But if you can get past all the testosterone, it's worth it.

I sat up because I was feeling slightly indignant, and I debate better in a vertical position. "You're the one," I pointed out, "who's always wrestling me down and saying, 'Ooh, baby, fuck me just one more time.' "

She laughed, not the least bit embarrassed by her lust. "Yeah, yeah, okay," she admitted. "But now, you know, I'd kinda like to be *seen* somewhere with you."

It was a funny way to put it, I thought, like I was someone to show off or display to her friends. Maybe no one believed that she was dating a forty-year-old. I know my friends found the situation slightly incredible. "No way!" Beth said when I told her. And yes, okay, I told her in the hope that she might leak the news to Claire. But Beth was more interested in whether Lexy might be a potential baby-sitter.

"You're not, like, ashamed to be going out with me, are you?" Lexy asked.

I couldn't admit to Lexy that she wasn't exactly my idea of mature. "Sexually open" was a better description of her. She had taught me more about sex in a couple of weeks than all ten of my lovers, women and men, combined. "Where do you want to go?" I asked.

"To the movies," Lexy said without skipping a beat. "Do you want to call one of your friends and invite them along? How about Harold? I'd like to meet him." She looked enthusiastic and hopeful, but Harold was the last person I would invite to join me and Lexy for anything. I just didn't trust him. I could picture him now, giving me knowing sidelong winks or making clucking noises in my ear.

"No, he's busy," I said a little too quickly. "I mean, he often goes out of town on Sundays."

I knew Lexy didn't believe me for a second, but thankfully she let it drop. Talking about Harold reminded me that I had promised to go with him to Chappaqua the following weekend without realizing which weekend it was. "Wait a minute," I said, jumping up to check my appointment book, "is next weekend Gay Pride?" I hadn't missed a Gay Pride march in fifteen years. Harold knew that and had completely taken advantage of my chronic problem of keeping track of dates without a calendar.

"Yeah," Lexy said, wriggling into her jeans. "Do you want to…."

She stopped and pulled on my T-shirt by mistake, which had been discarded with hers at the foot of the bed. "Oops, this is yours," she smiled, stripping it off again. She stood with only her jeans on, her beautiful full breasts facing me, with what had to be a difficult question for her. "Do you want to, you know, march together?"

"Unfortunately," I said, "I'll be out of town."

"You're going away Gay Pride weekend?" she asked, her voice dipping to a whisper. "Why are you going away Gay Pride weekend?"

I sat down again on the bed, wondering how I could squirm out of my promise to Harold. He surely knew what weekend it was; that was probably why he planned to come out to his family then. But dragging me into it unknowingly was cruel. "Harold isn't out to his family, and he asked me to go with him when he tells them he's gay," I explained. "I've gone with him there a few other times, kind of as…well, as a beard."

"A what?"

"A beard. You know, he's not out, so I play girlfriend."

"You're kidding." She sat down again too. "You pretend to be straight? I don't get it."

Neither, really, did I. I had been out to my own family for a dozen years. I got it over with at Christmas one year, when my parents and siblings were assembled and opening presents. None of them had met Claire, but they knew I lived with a woman whose name they all conveniently kept forgetting. My mother simply referred to her as "the other girl." "Are you bringing the other girl?" she asked on the phone when I mentioned what train I'd be taking to Connecticut. Claire refused to come to Christmas with me until I told them the truth about us. So that year I brazenly signed all their packages "Love, Lynn and Claire."

Everyone was ignoring the fact that I'd done this until my brother picked up his present. " 'Claire'?" Will said loudly. "Who the hell is Claire?" It was like a loud fart in the middle of a poetry reading.

"Oh, is that all?" Will said after I told them, to break the ice that had suddenly frozen the evening. "For a minute I was worried about you, Lynnie. I thought you were signing things from you and your *dog*."

"Don't ask me why I do it," I said to Lexy. "Harold's my best friend. I feel like he needs my help. And I have a hard time saying no to him."

"Even when he asks you to, well, *lie*?"

It was such an honest and horrified response, I wanted to cry. Lexy could see that I was upset, and she crawled across the bed and put her arms around me.

"I'm sorry, babe. I'm sorry," she said.

"I know it's a bad thing to help someone stay in the closet, but you don't really understand," I explained hurriedly and without really thinking. "It's been harder for people my age. It's so much easier for young lesbians to come out now. Your generation is more open and honest about their sexuality, but you have a lot less to lose."

"Oh, yeah," she said sarcastically, sitting back on her heels and staring at me in amazement, "it's *so* easy. That's why my friend Rob tried to kill himself when he was sixteen and why my roommate Marga's parents cut off her college funds junior year and she had to drop out and waitress full time. Hello! Do we live in the same country or what? I'm so sick of people *your* age reminding people my age that you paved the road to freedom for us."

I had never pushed the age thing so far with her, and she sounded thoroughly disgusted. And who could blame her? Wouldn't I have reacted the same way if someone sixty had said such condescending things to me?

It had been comforting to have her arms around me, and I wanted them back. "I'm sorry," I said sheepishly. "I'm sorry I was so arrogant." I leaned toward her, nuzzling her slightly, and her arms slid around me reluctantly, first one, then the other.

"You've got this really weird thing about age," she noted, and her hug was stiffer than it had been before.

Lexy was right, of course. It started the first time someone called me "ma'am" instead of "miss." Not that I'd ever really liked being addressed as "miss," but the passage to "ma'am" was a significant one. It was a particularly dramatic moment that I still remember. Sometime in my early thirties, when I had stopped being mistaken for a college student, I was buying *The New York Times* at my local combination magazine-newspaper-Lotto store, waiting for the clerk to change my five-dollar bill. Just then, a clean-cut college boy with a blond crew cut — the type of kid you expect to be a Christian fundamentalist, a neo-Nazi, the boy next door, or all three — approached the counter and glanced nervously at the clerk first, then at me, then back at the clerk. His mouth twitched a little. For a fleeting minute, I thought, *This is it, he's got a gun, we're all going to die* — not an uncommon thought for a New Yorker when someone looks so uneasy and shaky. Then the boy spoke: "Do you have any...do you have any...." He looked at me and gulped, then turned back to the clerk. "...do you have any *Screw?*" As the clerk handed me my change and reached down to get the pornography behind the counter, the young man faced me again with a flush of embarrassment. "Sorry, ma'am. I didn't mean to be...to be rude." It was such a bizarre moment, and my relief felt so complete that I didn't even notice I was shaking until I was out on the sidewalk.

After I calmed down, I wasn't sure why the boy had apologized, but I figured it was because he had cut in front of me while the clerk was making my change. When I repeated the incident to Claire, though, she had a different interpretation. "I think he was ashamed to be asking for *Screw* in front of a lady," she posited. "He called you 'ma'am,' after all. Maybe it was kind of like being caught by his teacher or his mother. Not just because it's porn but also because he had to say the name '*Screw*' in mixed company."

Her theory made more sense than mine, but it was the fact that she'd likened me to the boy's teacher or mother that stuck in my head and tormented me.

"He was probably nineteen," I protested. "There's no way I could be his mother! Unless I had him right after puberty."

"I know that, Lynnie, but let's say it's his first time buying porn. He works up his courage, walks right up to the clerk, then all of a sudden there's this woman at the counter. He doesn't even see her, really, just that she's female, and you're not supposed to say 'dirty' words in front of someone you address as 'ma'am.' "

"But people used to call me 'miss.' "

"Oh, people have been calling me 'ma'am' for at least three years. It's no big deal," she said to comfort me. "We're not kids anymore, you know." Claire should have given up when it was clear I'd missed her point.

"So," I said defensively, "you're saying you think I look like I could be his mother?"

My obsession with age worsened as my thirties went by, until I reached thirty-nine and a period of deep depression set in. I spent an entire year dreading forty, watching my friends hit it first, including

Claire six months before me. "How does it feel?" I asked her as I served her breakfast in bed that morning. I don't know what I expected as an answer.

"It feels just like yesterday," she replied casually. She had long since stopped indulging me in futile no-win conversations about age. On more than one occasion, she had even put me in my place, reminding me of the friends we'd lost to AIDS, all in their thirties. Or of Alec, who greeted his fortieth by saying with a big smile of relief, "I made it!" This would usually keep me from self-indulgence for a day or two; then I was back to my despair, counting each gray hair that popped out of my head and pointing it out to my besieged lover.

"Get your hair colored then, for God's sake," Claire finally snapped at me one day.

In retrospect I think something else was going on. Maybe subconsciously I knew that Claire and I had grown apart, two women who had been together since their late twenties and had less and less in common as they approached middle age. Without really realizing it, I was anticipating my biggest fear — spending my senior years alone in a tiny apartment in New York City.

I was on time for lunch with Jude, but she was a few minutes late, so I sat at the bar of the restaurant with a seltzer and a cigarette. New York has become slightly fascist about smoking, allowing it only in the bars and outdoor patios of restaurants. I knew it would be my last cigarette for a couple of hours, and I savored it.

"You smoke?" Jude commented before she even greeted me. My smoking was never an issue with Lexy, who went through a little over a pack a day herself.

"Well, I smoked during college and right after," I said, not really answering the question. As the hostess led us to our place, I enviously eyed the tables on the patio, where we weren't headed and where clouds of smoke drifted above the lunchers' heads.

Jude had already pronounced lunch her treat and had suggested a very chichi place in the Flatiron district called Bo's, where, by the look of the trendy decor, a midday meal was bound to cost twice as much as dinner at most places I was used to eating. The tables were set with very fine white linen, topped with brightly colored majolica plates and water and wine goblets of contrasting cobalt and cranberry glass. A sure sign of a snooty restaurant is a snooty waiter, and ours frowned and shook his head patronizingly when I ordered a glass of chardonnay with my entrée of grilled vegetables with smoked goat cheese.

"May I suggest the mmmermmj instead?" he sniffed, but I had never heard of that varietal, didn't catch its name, and just wanted him to go away so we could talk.

"No, the chardonnay will be fine," I insisted, and he rolled his eyes and went off to tell the other waiters about the commoners at table four.

"So," Jude continued, "you smoked a long time ago and—"

I noticed how she said "a long time ago" to refer to my college days. I wasn't fooling Ms. Vassar about my age for a minute.

"And then I started again just recently. After about fourteen years."

"Why?" she said, wrinkling her eyebrows. She was so clean and refined, I bet she never let a cigarette come within twenty feet of her.

"I was going through some shit," I said. "A sort of messy breakup."

"Oh, *those,*" she nodded knowingly. "Those can be torture. I broke up with someone not very long ago too."

I wasn't interested in going this route with her any more than I had wanted to pursue it with Lexy, so I tried to segue into another topic. "Speaking of breakups, Ross's leaving April was a shock. What's the real story there?"

Our waiter plunked down a liter bottle of Saratoga water and poured some for each of us. "I'm not sure what you mean," Jude said with hesitation.

"I just always thought there was more going on there than April admitted," I noted.

Jude looked overly self-conscious as she took a drink of water, as if afraid of dribbling down her chin. "Oh, no. They're both just flirtatious that way; there wasn't anything going on," Jude said, arching forward. "Actually...well, the truth is, I dated Ross...for about six months."

I tried to look casual and cool, but my eyes felt like huge saucers. *You're kidding* was on my lips, but I didn't say it. What *could* I say? I took a sip of wine. My gaydar, I thought immediately, wasn't just aging: It needed a major tune-up.

"Ross pretty much turned me off men for good," she added quickly, and I saw our waiter smirk as he laid out our orders. "I don't know what I was thinking to let myself be taken in by a man again, and one that was younger than me at that."

Her apparent sexual confusion was foreign to me, because I'd been confident of my orientation for almost twenty years. College was a big blur, and thankfully so. I'd spent the first three years in school trying to make it work with a couple of egotistical young men, then spent my senior year in bewildered and painful celibacy. I kept journals that agonized over my crushes on women friends, but I never had the courage or self-knowledge to act on my desires. So while other people reminisced about their college days as golden years, I viewed them as an ordeal that I couldn't wait to put behind me.

"Don't think badly of me," Jude said suddenly, pushing a roasted pepper listlessly around her plate, "because I went out with Ross. I can tell you don't care much for him." She said it in such a plaintive tone that I couldn't help but take pity on her.

"Believe me, I've made my share of mistakes," I snickered. "I think the main reason I find Ross so unbearable doesn't really have a lot to do with him. It's just that he reminds me of the arrogant boys I dated in college."

"You dated men too?" I was instantly glad I'd said it, because her whole body seemed to relax. Throughout the talk about Ross, Jude had been hunched forward, tight and pinched like she was being squeezed in a vise, and she suddenly leaned back against her chair and speared a piece of eggplant with unexpected gusto.

"Oh, sure," I said. "Most lesbians have, at one time or another. It's our social conditioning. The trick," I added with a wink over the Saratoga bottle, "is knowing when to stop."

As intended, the quip made her smile and blush a little. It got us over the hump of discomfort and unfamiliarity. I ordered a second glass of wine as we lingered over our entrées. After, I realized we never got around to the stated purpose of the meeting, to talk about writing as a career. Jude seemed to have forgotten that it had been on her agenda.

That evening at 6, still feeling the effects of a prolonged lunch with two full glasses of wine, I met Claire at Jocelyn Truitt's law office in a brownstone on West Twentieth Street. The bell for Apartment 1 said "J. Truitt and C. Gusso," and I pushed that first before noticing that the one for Apartment 2 read "Truitt and Gusso, Attorneys-at-Law." The two seemed to be both law partners *and* domestic partners. The situation held all the warning signals of lesbian fusion, that unpleasant condition in which the partners in a couple begin to think, sound, and look alike. Given that I considered fusion a sort of character flaw, I tried to keep an open mind about Jocelyn Truitt's ability to effectively mediate my relationship with my ex-lover.

Counselor Truitt was nearing fifty, a short, butchy woman with a raspy voice who looked peculiar in a woman's suit and strand of pearls. Office drag, I thought, as much a costume as if she were an actor playing a role.

"Ms. Woods, it's nice to meet you," she greeted me. I wondered how much Claire had told her and what our mediator thought of me at first glance. During our breakup I had consented to visit Claire's therapist, Laurel, with her for a couple of sessions to ease our "adjustment," but I had instantly judged her to be too much on Claire's side and left in an annoyed huff in the middle of the first hour. I was fully prepared for a repetition of that experience.

"Thanks for agreeing to come to my office. I thought it would be cozier here than in a public space."

Cozier? I didn't expect to be having tea and cookies with her and Claire. Truitt had arranged a friendly circle of armchairs at one end of her spacious and well-appointed office, looking out onto the patio and garden below, just beginning to bloom with red and yellow roses. But I wasn't fooled by the cordial atmo- sphere. I was sure Claire wanted blood.

"Please, Ms. Woods, have a seat and get comfortable. Ms. Ulrich called a little while ago and will be a few minutes late." Truitt stood looking at me oddly, as if she thought she had to entertain me before Claire arrived. "Do you mind if I just take care of a few items on my desk?"

I was relieved that she left me alone; her overattentiveness was making me more nervous than I had been before I arrived. While she rustled some papers, I pulled a book out of my bag and tried unsuccessfully to concentrate on it. In preparation for writing April's book, I was forcing myself to read a lot of antifeminist diatribes with their accompanying feminist responses. I was midway through Katie Roiphe's *The Morning After* but found it so badly argued that I couldn't bear to read more than a few pages at a time.

I glanced through a section decrying campus hysteria over "alleged" date rapes and put it back into my bag.

Truitt didn't have any magazines in her office, so I read her diplomas instead, just to do something while I waited. I had a habit of doing this in doctors' offices too, just to assure myself that they knew what they were up to. Barnard, BA, 1970. NYU, JD, 1973. ABA accreditation, 1974. She had probably passed the bar exam on the first try, a real feat in New York State. Beneath her diplomas were two framed color photographs, one of her shaking hands with former mayor David Dinkins and one with Hillary Clinton. *At least she's a Democrat and proud of it,* I thought.

I glanced over at Truitt and found, to my embarrassment, that she was watching me study her credentials. "Everything look okay to you?" she asked with a sharp grin.

"I didn't like my book," I explained, blushing, "and I needed something to read."

Uh-oh, I thought, *she's already got my number.*

Thankfully Claire buzzed at that moment, and Truitt went to let her in. I hadn't seen my ex-lover in almost four months, and the sight of her was something of a shock. Years ago, in her early thirties, Claire's long black hair had grayed prematurely and become a stunning mix of silver with black accent strands. She had always worn it pulled back in a braid to keep it out of her way. To highlight her hair she had preferred black clothing and had more black turtlenecks than anyone I had ever met. Her style had always seemed like mine, stuck somewhere in the late '70s or early '80s.

She was completely remade, as if she were the "after" in a series of before-and-after shots. Her hair was cropped into a fetching and expensive-looking cut that reminded me of Demi Moore's in *Ghost.* The cotton turtlenecks were replaced by a rich cerise silk shirt worn over flowing black pants. And most surprising, when I brushed her cheek with a sisterly kiss, I could smell the trace of some sweet flowery oil on her skin.

"Claire," I said, trying not to stare. "You look…great."

"I had my color chart done," she smiled. "I realized there were a lot of colors I was missing out on."

I noticed that she didn't say anything complimentary about my appearance, which was pretty much as it had always been — button-down shirt, vest, trousers, all in various nondescript neutrals.

"If you want," she suggested, "I'll give you the woman's number who color-analyzed me. I have a feeling you're a winter, and you should be wearing brighter colors too."

After these pleasantries, you can imagine how much I was looking forward to our mediation session. I was a frump next to my elegant ex-girlfriend, who looked every inch like an art director. And Jocelyn Truitt, who had never met Claire in person before, couldn't seem to take her eyes off her.

"Well, ladies," Truitt began. (Let me say that I hate it when someone addresses me as a "lady.") "Shall we start? Let's all take a seat and get comfortable."

Truitt was into comfort, I could tell, since it was the second time she'd mentioned it since I'd arrived. Comfortable was the last thing I felt. I was squirming in my seat before we'd even started.

"I'd like to do an intake first," Truitt announced. "I know some of the particulars of your request for mediation, but I'd like to hear them firsthand from each of you. Ms. Ulrich, since you made the initial inquiry, would you like to start?"

"Call me Claire," Claire said sweetly. "Well, as I mentioned to you earlier, Lynn and I broke up about four months ago after being together thirteen years. It was quite traumatic for both of us, but it seemed like a necessary step. We had stopped growing together and were really just growing apart." Claire talked directly to Truitt, avoiding my eyes. Her voice wavered a little in a way that seemed genuine. "It's difficult when you get together in your mid twenties and then you hit forty and find you're different people than you were." She had said this all to me before, so it wasn't news how she felt.

"I was the one who initiated the breakup," Claire went on.

Yes, I thought snidely, *you're the dumper and I'm the dumpee.*

"So even though it's been hard for both of us, I think Lynn has taken it particularly badly — you know, not really wanting to get on with things."

"Objection!" I cried, forgetting I wasn't on trial.

"Ms. Woods, let's just finish hearing Claire's comments and then we'll go right to yours. Is that okay?"

"Call me Lynn," I muttered begrudgingly.

"So my feeling is that Lynn is having some problems," Claire continued, "which is fine, but I've suspected her of some weird behavior lately." She stopped and lowered her eyes.

"Could you define 'weird'?" Truitt pursued. *Weird,* I wanted to scream, *is me sitting here listening to this.*

"Well, I think she's been calling my apartment late at night and hanging up," Claire said quickly. "I've been receiving lots of magazines I never ordered, things Lynn would know I'd hate. I also seem to have gotten onto some pretty disturbing mailing lists. And then, someone buzzed my apartment in the middle of the night. I was terrified, so I changed my phone to an unlisted one and didn't give Lynn the number. The harassment stopped. I reported it all to the Anti-Violence Project."

"Why do you think it might be Ms. Woods — Lynn — who is

doing the harassing?" Truitt said, holding her chin in her hand in what looked like mock concern to me.

"I just have a feeling," Claire said. "Look, you live with someone for thirteen years, you get to know them very well. Lynn was extremely troubled when I moved out, crying nonstop and constantly pressing me for information about whether or not I was seeing someone else. Then, after all that time together, she said she never wanted to see me again. It was just plain hurtful. I don't think phone harassment or dirty tricks are beyond her, I really don't."

Truitt shook her head knowingly. That must have said it all to her. What normal lesbian *doesn't* keep in touch with all her ex-lovers?

"Excuse me," I said, abruptly breaking in, "do I ever get to say anything, or have I just been tried and convicted?"

"Lynn, this is mediation, not a trial," Truitt assured me. "We're here to listen to both sides and reach some sort of resolution."

"So do I get to talk now?" I repeated.

"Of course."

"First of all," I started, feeling my adrenaline rush, "I *have* been getting on with my life, thank you very much. Though I have to tell you it's hard after someone's completely devastated you." Claire looked at her feet, which were nicely shod in sleek feminine slip-ons with thin socks that matched her shirt perfectly. She used to wear oxfords with white athletic socks, but if you're going to go femme, hey, why not go all the way?

"In fact, I've been seeing *two* women," I announced proudly, with heavy emphasis on the "two." My revelation produced the desired effect. Truitt sat up straighter and seemed to listen more attentively, and Claire turned toward me in amazement.

"Two?" she asked.

"Yes, two. So much for your theory that I somehow need to harass you because I'm pathetic and have no life. Believe me, I have a lot to do late at night." By this point I was so good, I convinced *myself* I had never made a crank call to Claire.

"I asked Beth if you were seeing anybody, and she mentioned one, not *two*," Claire said skeptically. But then she realized what this last admission meant.

"So it's all right for you to inquire about *my* love life but not okay for me to want to know about *yours*. Do I understand this right?" I demanded.

"Look, my asking Beth is totally different..." Claire was on her feet, hands on her shapely hips. I stood up to face her eye to furious eye.

"Oh, yeah? Tell me how. Just tell me how!"

"I don't have to tell you anything!"

"Ladies..." By now Truitt had lost total control. In fact, I think we had both forgotten she was there. We were back in time, about ten years old, and we were in a schoolyard fight that, at any minute, was going to disintegrate into pushing. "Ladies, please, our job here—"

"This is pointless," Claire said, so hot and bothered that steam could have come out of her ears. "This is absolutely fucking pointless. You will never ever admit you've done anything wrong. You win! Our relationship was perfect, you're perfect, and everything is all my fault!" And before Truitt had time to call us "ladies" again, Claire had stormed out of the office in a color-coordinated huff.

"Well," I said, picking up my bag and getting ready to leave too, "I hope your other mediations have gone smoother than this one." I felt suddenly sorry for Truitt because she seemed so at a loss for words or actions.

"Sometimes there's just too much anger," Truitt finally concluded, but her eyes were wide as saucers. "At the next session we'll have two mediators present, and maybe you and Claire could—"

"I don't *think* so," I said. "These two *ladies* aren't going to be in the same room together anytime soon. But thanks anyway. It's not your fault." I patted her arm because I didn't know how else to say goodbye.

Out on the front stoop, I lit a cigarette and glanced toward Seventh Avenue. Claire was at the corner — who could miss that cerise shirt? — waving frantically for a cab. I think our fight had really shaken her up but good, probably more than all the telephone hang-ups and even the 3 A.M. buzzing at her apartment door. It was odd, but even though I seemed to have achieved a small triumph, I didn't feel vindicated in the least.

That was when the craziness started.

The mediation session with Claire felt like the final split, even though we'd separated months earlier. I guess I had never realized until that point just how much I wanted to hurt Claire because she had hurt me. Perverse, I know — the dumpee lashes back, becoming even worse than the dumper. Well, like I said earlier, it's hard to be gracious when your heart's been flattened. I had fully intended to be amiable and accommodating in my meeting with Claire, maybe even own up to my telephone behavior and, of all things, apologize. But seeing how completely she had remade herself, almost as if trying to escape the old Claire, my lover, broke open all the old wounds.

I got home from Jocelyn Truitt's that evening much earlier than expected, and I immediately called Lexy. "Can you come over tonight?" I coaxed in my sexiest voice. "I want to fuck you like you wouldn't *believe*." After just a few weeks, I knew what worked with Lexy. She was practically out the door before we hung up.

Then, calculating how long it would take Lexy to get to my place from her apartment in Little Italy — and subtracting twenty minutes, in case she was so wet she sprang for a cab — I called Jude.

"Lynn!"

I was still in my sex-kitten mode. "I just wanted to tell you again...how much *fun* I had at lunch," I said. "And that I'm hoping we can get together again...really soon." The pauses were deliberate, a little breathy, and maybe just a trace too Marilyn Monroe-like, but I didn't care. I suspected that Jude was feeling the initial rush of getting a call from a prospect so soon after the first "date."

"There's a benefit at the community center Monday night to kick off Gay Pride Week," she said quickly. "Jill donates money there, so she got two tickets, but she's not going to use them. Would you like to go?"

"That sounds great, but I had something sooner in mind," I said playfully. "Like tomorrow night." I had my week-at-a-glance book open in front of me, with LEXY written in big black letters over Wednesday and now Thursday nights. My pen was poised to mark JUDE over Friday. "Maybe dinner? A movie?"

"I had something planned, but I can get out of it," Jude replied. I could hear the rustling pages of her date book at the other end of the line as she figured out when she could see whomever she was canceling for me. "I'd *much* rather see you."

Bingo, I thought.

As we were hanging up, Lexy rang the buzzer downstairs.

By now you probably think I'm making this all up. When I look back it does seem a little like a forty-year-old lesbian's wet dream — two beautiful young women clamoring to get into her bed, while scores of other cooler and groovier women — and men — are left

72

in the dust. If I were a person who wore hats, I think I would have found that my head had grown a few sizes that summer.

An hour or so after Lexy arrived, we were sprawled on the floor of the living room with a bowl of popcorn I had microwaved and accidentally burned. I'm not really that bad in the kitchen, but I was still wearing the strap-on while I was making the popcorn, and I think I got distracted by the way it bobbed when I moved. *No wonder men's minds are always on their dicks,* I thought.

The living room rug was Lexy's favorite spot for sex — a bit of a nuisance because I'd never been very keen on vacuuming, and now I had to do it a couple of times a week. My mother, a woman who spent the better part of her adulthood religiously vacuuming every Wednesday and Saturday morning, would have been horrified to learn that it was only the prospect of a hot time on the rug that got her older daughter's Hoover out of storage.

I was stretched out, warmly remembering our sexual exploits of just minutes before when, "I can't stay," Lexy announced suddenly, picking through the bowl for the lighter, fluffier kernels.

She had always stayed over when we had a date, so I was understandably confused. It didn't even occur to me when I called and blurted out my needs to her over the phone that she might have something else to do that night.

But the unspoken rule of our relationship was "No strings," and I had just come from a harrowing session with Claire in which I was reminded of the way I grilled her for information when we were breaking up. So I plopped a couple of pieces of popcorn into my mouth and said casually, "Okay."

"Okay?" Lexy repeated.

"Sure, okay," I said. "I realize this date was pretty spontaneous. I'm not going to flatter myself that I'm the only person in your date book."

"You don't want to know what I'm doing?" she asked dubiously.

"Only if you want to tell me," I said. Actually, my ego was dying to know. But I reminded myself that I didn't want an exclusive relationship with Lexy or any 23-year-old, especially not now, with Jude — the 25-year-old! — on the horizon.

"Huh," she said, running her hand through the leftovers in the bowl and bringing it out empty. "Well, it's just that I promised to have dinner with my brother, Hart, who's in town on business."

"Oh," I said, a little disappointed. I had half imagined her dashing crosstown from our rendezvous to one with another older woman. "What does he do?"

"He sells something or other," she said without interest. "I can't remember what. Some kind of, like, software or something." Lexy bit her lip and watched me coyly from behind a wave of auburn hair. "You wouldn't want to come, would you? To dinner, I mean."

"Now *there's* an invitation!" I said sarcastically.

"No, really, I mean it. It would be great if you'd join us. He's not bad really. He has his own amateur rock band in Chicago." She rolled onto her stomach, a position she knew had recently begun to drive me wild with desire. "Later we could come back here."

"Thanks," I replied, "but I think I'll pass on the software salesman slash rock musician." When she looked hurt I added quickly, "I really have to do some work. I lost a lot of time today in meetings."

"Who'd you meet with?" she asked, pulling on her T-shirt. It seemed like a natural question, unless we expected to show no interest whatsoever in each other's lives.

"Oh, my boss's new assistant," I added nonchalantly. "She had some, uh, paperwork for me to sign." I really didn't want to discuss either Jude or Claire. "And then I just had some other people to meet with related to work. All pretty boring. So tonight I should hit the computer."

"Okay," she said with a little pout. Then with a spurt of hope, "How about tomorrow? I know a party we could go to after work."

We still hadn't ventured out much in public together, just once to the movies and once for Indian food. We hadn't met each other's friends, though Lexy begged to meet mine. Hers, I didn't have much interest in. One Lexy at a time was about all I could handle.

Besides, tomorrow was Jude.

"I can't tomorrow," I said quickly. "Maybe Saturday after you get off?"

"What're you doing tomorrow?" This seemed much more intrusive and not just an I-need-something-to-talk-about-while-I'm-getting-dressed kind of question.

"Oh, I don't know," I answered evasively. "Dinner with a friend."

"There's that nameless 'friend' again," she laughed, but I could tell she wasn't amused. She almost poked her toes right through her sock, she pulled it on so fiercely.

"Oh, come on," I said, opening my date book a crack so she could see her name written everywhere. "Here you are, every other day of the week. LEXY. LEXY. LEXY. What more could a girl want?"

"Who's Jude?" she asked, ignoring my question as she spotted Jude's name on Friday night. Luckily it wasn't in caps, though I had scrawled it in red ink and even underlined it.

"The friend," I replied, slapping the book closed again. "I've...I've known him for years. We haven't seen each other in a long time, and now we're sort of rediscovering each other."

The "him" seemed to relieve her. She knew it wasn't going to be a man who came between us. *Thank God*, I thought, *for androgynous names*.

Lexy opened my date book again and wrote her own name on Saturday, so big and bold that nothing else could have fit in the block if I'd tried. "Just don't ever lie to me," she warned as she slid a finger down my cheek.

Now I was really starting to worry.

That was the night I got late-night hang-ups. They happened after 11, in almost the same way I had called Claire in months past just to see if she was home. Except whoever called me seemed to be a pro — they phoned twice in rapid succession, as if to punctuate my fear. "Who the hell is this?" I screamed into the phone after the second call, but my terror was answered with only a calm, cool, calculated click. It was eerily coincidental, and my paranoia made me believe I was being paid back for Claire — what goes around, comes around, literally. After the calls I wished I *had* gone to dinner with Lexy and her brother, just so she would have come home with me that night. I was starting not to want to sleep alone.

I dreamed I was at a conference naked. It was some very important feminist shindig, and April Ronsard and Jill Womann and Gloria Steinem and all the other big girls were there. No one would tell me where my clothes were, but they all seemed to know. They simply pointed at me and shook their heads while they whispered to each other behind their hands. Claire, arrayed in flowing purple silk, was invited to sit at the big-girl table, but I was forced to hide in a stall in the bathroom, waiting for some kind person to bring me my clothes.

"That's fascinating," Jude remarked the next night while we were on line for the movies. "You dreamed about Jill?"

"Well, she was there," I said. I hadn't emphasized her mother's role in my dream, but Jude had picked up on it as the one thing that really intrigued her. "It really was more about nakedness."

"Hmm," Jude said, but I could tell I had already lost her interest. Who *doesn't* dream about nakedness and exposure? I wasn't as fascinating as I hoped I'd be.

It was probably not the best choice for a date — some romantic comedy starring Gwyneth Paltrow would have been better — but we went to see a documentary about Leni Riefenstahl, the filmmaker who created the Nazi propaganda film *Triumph of the Will*. The problem with Riefenstahl was that she has never acknowledged her own culpability in the Nazi war machine. Today she still maintains that *Triumph of the Will* was art, not politics.

All the way through the documentary, I kept thinking how much Lexy would have liked seeing a film about a filmmaker and that I hadn't thought clearly enough when I suggested it to Jude. I was already getting my women confused. Jude started yawning about halfway through the three-hour epic and after, when we were out on the sidewalk, asked if sometime soon I'd like to go see *Mr. Wrong*.

While I lit a cigarette in front of Film Forum, a white-haired woman with a cane who looked a little lost wandered up to us and stared directly into Jude's face. I expected her to inquire about directions or the time. "Can I ask you, what did you think of that movie?" she said pointedly.

"Well," Jude replied with a cautious glance at me, "it was a little long and kind of depressing. I mean, Riefenstahl's such a big liar."

The woman nodded furiously and stabbed the air with her finger. "My point exactly!" she barked. "The reviews said it was *funny!*

Hysterical, they said. Can you imagine? I thought it was the most depressing movie I ever saw. That, that Leni who's-it has no *shame!*"

The woman turned away from us without asking my opinion and interrogated a straight couple coming out of the theater. "Can I ask you a question?" she said to them.

"Maybe she's a plant for some public survey on movies," I suggested. As we walked off down the block, we heard a man's voice comment, "Kind of long, I'd say, and a little depressing." We made a teasing bet about how many moviegoers she would survey before she was satisfied that enough people had concurred with her. I guessed five, and Jude picked ten.

"But we'll never know who won," Jude observed. "We'd have to wait at the theater until she leaves."

"Oh, I'm sure I won," I said with a confident smirk. "I'm very good at things like this."

"Oh, yeah? So, then, what's the prize?" As we walked along, she was casually bumping into me, nudging my arm with hers and blinking at me behind long lashes. I decided to take the plunge.

"You are," I grinned lewdly. "I won, and you have to give yourself to me." I surprised even myself with my raunchy boldness.

You've gotten good at this, I thought.

Jude didn't have any sex toys. In fact, I discovered on our way to her apartment that she'd never spent the night with a woman before. She'd had some mutual masturbation sessions with a friend at Vassar, but they'd been too nervous to take their clothes off.

"I guess that makes me a virgin," Jude said provocatively. "Just an innocent young thing for you to take advantage of."

Well, that was hardly true, since besides Ross she'd dated a half-dozen other young men. But she seemed to like the role, so we went with it.

"This is some place," I commented when we got to her apartment in the West Sixties. We reached the fourth floor in a rich, mahogany-lined elevator. The living room was a cavernous space with a cathedral ceiling and spectacular windows. A kitchen, dining room, and small study occupied the far end of the space, opposite the windows, and above those rooms a staircase led to a second level. I was just about to ask where a 25-year-old personal assistant gets the dough for such prime Manhattan real estate when Jude answered my question.

"It's Jill's," she said, bringing me a glass of wine. "She used to work and live here and go to her place upstate at the end of the week. But in the last few years she moved up there full-time and hardly ever comes down except for openings. She even pays the utilities and maid service. I get to live for free, which is lucky, considering how badly April pays me. If I had to live on my salary, I'd be sharing some roach-infested place with three roommates."

"Who would have thought there'd be so much money," I quipped, "in carving wooden pussies?"

"There isn't, really," Jude corrected me with a laugh. "She's made some good sales but not until she stopped doing 'women's art' in the '80s. Mostly she invested really well in other people's stuff. She and my father bought this place in the early 1960s, before Lincoln Center was finished and no one wanted to live around here. These apartments were originally low-income artists' studios in the early 1900s. Hence, the high ceiling and windows."

"Did you live here when you were growing up?" I asked. The main space was dotted with Jill Womann sculptures and paintings that had to be original Lee Krasners and Helen Frankenthalers and Judy Chicagos. Even the chairs and tables seemed to be works of art that didn't look very inviting.

"Yeah," she replied, amused. "But I never appreciated it then. There were too many artsy-fartsy types in and out all the time."

"So you have this incredible space all to yourself?" I asked in amazement. My entire apartment would have fit into one corner.

"Well, it's not like the place is mine or anything," she countered. "I mean, yeah, I live here, and yeah, it's huge — but it's *hers*." The resentful way she said "hers" shut me up immediately. We were treading on shaky ground, I could tell. World travel courtesy of Famous Mom. Job courtesy of Famous Mom. Fabulous apartment courtesy of Famous Mom. *But,* I thought, *if Jude wanted her own life so desperately, couldn't she just do it instead of resenting her privilege?*

"What's upstairs?" I asked suddenly to switch gears.

"The bedrooms," she said. "The master suite and two smaller rooms, including one that was mine growing up. I use the one that used to be the guest bedroom. I couldn't deal with having the same room I had as a kid."

"You mean you didn't take over the master suite the minute she moved out?" I said, astonished. "I would have been in there so fast—"

"Well," Jude said quickly, "I always *fuck* in there. I just sleep in the other room."

"Show me," I said, and we left the lights downstairs blazing all night long.

There were six messages on my answering machine, five of which

80

were hang-ups. The sixth was from Lexy, who, I could tell, was smoking while she left the message.

"Guess who?" she said caustically. "I guess Jude had a sex reassignment — isn't that what you call it? — overnight."

The message spooked me, and I erased it immediately. I was just about to call up Lexy and tell her to leave me the fuck alone when the phone rang.

"I apologize," she said softly. "It was rude to leave that message. I was just mad that you'd lied to me."

"Were all those hang-ups you too?" I demanded.

"No! I wouldn't do that," she insisted. "That's creepy."

"Look, Lexy, we're just dating," I said. "We never made any promises. We never said anything about being exclusive. You have no right to interfere in the rest of my life." Pretty harsh, but she had taken one step too far. Besides, I could afford to be cruel. Sex with Jude had been outstandingly inventive, especially after I found the cucumber in the refrigerator and Ross's leftover condoms in a drawer.

Lexy was quiet except for the soft sounds of smoking into the receiver.

"So, what, did you follow me?" I asked.

"You think I'm, like, a psychopath, don't you?" she said. "I was *at* the fucking movie. That's a movie I wanted to see with *you,* if you remember."

"Oh," I said, embarrassed. Of course — I had heard about the movie from Lexy, and that's why she had come to mind while I was watching it. Not only was I old but I was suffering from acute memory loss. Maybe dating two women at one time was too difficult a balancing act.

"Who is she?" Lexy cross-examined me. "She looks like a fucking *debutante*." That was probably the worst thing she could think of to call anyone her own age.

"She's just someone I work with," I answered.

"Oh, right. Someone you work with. Duh! You work at *home*, Lynn. You're a freelancer."

I had been foolish to take Jude to that particular movie, but I didn't have to tolerate this verbal abuse from Lexy. "Look, Lexy, I don't want to discuss it, okay? I'm not lying to you. You don't really understand how I work."

"No," she agreed with a snide laugh, "I guess I don't."

"Let's talk some other time," I suggested, purposely vague. Maybe I could get off the phone and call NYNEX to change my number.

"Okay, but...are we still on for tonight?" Lexy asked, her tone completely softened. I had totally forgotten that I was supposed to meet her that night after her waitressing shift at P.J.'s. Did she want to see me just to continue to torture me about Jude, or was her phone harangue all that was in store? I didn't want to risk it.

"I'm not sure that's a good idea...." I hesitated. A night at home alone seemed suddenly attractive. "Maybe we should cool it...."

"Come on, please?"

I've never been particularly adept at breakups over the phone, so I agreed to keep our date that night. *One last time,* I thought.

82

Jude and I were walking to my apartment on a clear, mild Monday night with lots of stars. We'd been to the Lesbian and Gay Community Services Center's annual Garden Party — not really a garden party at all but a block party that traditionally kicks off Gay Pride Week. West Thirteenth Street in the Village is cordoned off with blue police barriers, and neighbors hang out windows and off fire escapes watching a few thousand gay people sing and dance in the street.

It had been a particularly fun evening, since Harold was one of the numerous performers on the bill. On and off for years, his drag alter ego has been a ravishing creature named Freda Chews, who sings big-band tunes in a throaty contralto with a backup group called the Pride Boys. The Pride Boys have changed over time, two of the originals having died and been replaced by younger ones. I hadn't heard Freda perform in a couple of years, so it was a treat to see her strutting her stuff across the outdoor stage in three-inch heels and a clingy, black, sequined gown slit right up the side to her waist.

"Is this how you're going to tell your folks?" I asked Harold after

Freda's set. "Show up on their doorstep as their long-lost daughter, Freda Chews? Why don't you bring the Pride Boys instead of me?"

It was a joke, but he looked as if he were seriously considering it. "Hey, that's not a bad idea," he mused. "Go right for the jugular."

After I introduced Jude, Harold held his beaded bag to the side of his face and winked at me behind it. "What are you," he whispered, "some kind of babe magnet?" Then, thankfully, Freda had to go greet her fans.

It was a long and leisurely walk to my apartment, so I decided to broach a subject that had been on my mind since Lexy's annoying phone call the week before. "There's something I should tell you," I said to Jude with a cigarette dangling from my mouth, very Humphrey Bogart. "Only because I really like you, and we're having a good time. I don't want to get off on the wrong foot."

"What is it?" Jude looked concerned, and I realized my announcement must have sounded ominous. Once, long before I met Claire, a woman I was hoping to have sex with approached me with the same statement, and it had turned out she identified as bisexual. It was no big deal for me, but a few lesbians she'd dated had been distrustful of her because of it. I was glad her "confession" was something so minor: For a few excruciatingly long minutes, I had worried that she was going to say we couldn't have sex.

"I'm dating someone else too," I blurted out. "I thought it might be over with her, but it isn't." My intentions of breaking up with Lexy had been good, but my continuing desire to have sex with her won out. Besides, since our spat on the phone, Lexy had been a model of restraint and coolness. "I just thought you'd want to know," I continued. "I mean, I want to keep seeing both of you. But I know it's important to some women to be exclusive. I was monogamous for thirteen years with my last lover, and I'm just not ready for anything that intense again."

Jude sighed with relief, grabbed me by both shoulders, and kissed me. My instincts made me glance around nervously to see if anyone was going to run up and bash us for daring to be openly lesbian on the street. "I thought you were going to say it was already over with us," she smiled broadly. "Don't scare me like that!"

"So it's okay with you? We can just proceed from here?"

"Sure," she said. "I mean, come on, Lynn, we've only had two dates. I don't have any claim on you."

Good girl, I thought. This was exactly what I wanted from my two girlfriends. No rules, no strings, no games. Maybe I should introduce Jude to Lexy so she could teach her a few things about being casual.

But before I could thank her for her unusual openness, Jude was already shattering my illusion of the true fuck buddy. "Just tell me one thing," she asked slowly as we approached the Flatiron Building and the site of our two-hour lunch.

I held my breath, waiting to hear her request to see whether I could reasonably answer it. "You can ask me anything," I allowed, "but I can't promise you an answer. Fire away."

"Okay," Jude said carefully. "Okay." How many times could she say "okay"? "I was wondering — I mean — okay, who is she?"

Gay Pride Week was a nightmare from my perspective. Starting with Monday night, I had written JUDE and LEXY across alternating evenings in my date book. The nights started to blur together. No matter how many times I adjusted the station, every time I turned around, my radio was switched from National Public Radio (my preference) to either rap (Lexy's) or rock (Jude's). One particularly sticky moment was when Lexy showed up at my place and I hadn't had a chance to change the sheets from a date with Jude. Lexy tried not to sulk in the living room while I pulled out my other set of sheets and stripped the bed. After that I insisted that all dates with Jude be at her apartment.

I was so overly occupied with dating, I missed everything that was going on in the world. By the weekend I was exhausted and actually looking forward to a good old family party in the suburbs.

"I've got to hand it to you," Harold said when he picked me up on Sunday morning in a sleek rented red convertible. Besides door-to-door service, I had also insisted on a whole-wheat bagel with low-fat cream cheese and a tall, skinny mochaccino. "In all my years in action, I never got laid every single night of the week."

"Like I believe that," I scoffed.

"Honest," he insisted. "My best week ever — *ever*, mind you — was five nights out of seven. And that was way back in 1978. You, my little kumquat, should have been born a gay man."

"Speaking of gay men," I said, changing the subject, "let's hear the speech you're going to give the Fine family."

"Haven't got one," he said through a bite of bagel.

"You don't know what you're going to say?" I asked incredulously. "We're going to Bubbe's ninetieth birthday so you can come out, and you haven't got your speech on note cards?"

"I want it to be spontaneous. I want it to be what I feel at that moment."

"What if what you feel is scared shitless and words escape you?"

"Then," he smiled sheepishly, "that's where you come in."

"Oh, no, Harold!" I protested. "I'm already doing you this enormous favor, giving up Gay Pride to go to a Jewish family party in Westchester. I am not — I repeat, *not* — going to come out for you too!"

"You couldn't just help a little?" he pleaded. "Start things off somehow? Come out first?"

"They aren't my family; they're yours! I don't *have* to come out to them." I had spilled some of my mochaccino foam on the console in my rage, and I was trying to mop it up with one pathetic paper napkin while juggling the drippy cup. "How do you envision this? We're leaving, and I casually say, 'Oh, thank you, Mrs. Fine, and by the way, Harold and I won't be getting married after all because I'm gay'?"

"You could add, 'And he is too,' " Harold suggested.

"That's it! Let me out of this fucking car! The deal's off." We were traveling about fifty up the Henry Hudson Parkway, so my plea to be let out on the side of the road was as impractical as Harold's request that I come out to his family for him. But he managed to squeeze past several cars and pull to an abrupt halt on the shoulder while cars raced by us so fast, it felt like our aerodynamic convertible was going to be lifted off the ground.

"Okay," he said. "Go ahead, get out." When I didn't budge, he leaned over me and opened the door on the passenger side. "Go on, I haven't got all day."

I grabbed the handle and pulled the door roughly closed.

"Smart ass," I muttered, tearing into my bagel. "Just drive, okay?"

Fine family parties, I have come to learn, are always held at Aunt Miriam and Uncle Jack's. Uncle Jack is Harold's father's older brother, and Bubbe, Jack's mother, has lived with them for years in her own apartment, which they constructed especially for her in "the west wing." Aunt Miriam and Uncle Jack have a semipalatial mock-Tudor home on a few rolling acres in Chappaqua, complete with swimming pool and tennis court. For years Uncle Jack owned a very successful string of leather-goods stores in Manhattan and always gave Harold the richest, most expensive-looking briefcases, belts, and wallets. The last time I visited, Jack gave me a beautiful butter-soft purse, but since I never use purses, I gave it to my mother for Christmas.

"Harold!" Aunt Miriam greeted him with a big hug. "Dear!" she said, pecking me on the cheek. No matter how many times I visited her home, Aunt Miriam always managed to forget my name, and I often joked with Harold that she was probably too used to referring to me as "the shiksa" when I wasn't around. I waited for her to ask me how my plans for religious conversion were coming along, but she was wrapped up in her favorite nephew.

"Harold, your cousin Allan came all the way from Boston, can you believe it? With his darling new wife. She's a rabbi's daughter! You have to meet her." She dragged Harold away as he waved sheepishly at me over his shoulder.

Needless to say, Aunt Miriam was not too happy that Harold was "dating" a Christian and always made it very clear to both of us. But since I was neither dating Harold nor a practicing Christian, I just let it roll off my back and made my way to the festivities outside on the patio.

"Lynn, I'm glad you could come! Where's Harold?" Uncle Jack cared less about my conversion to Judaism than his wife did and always greeted me warmly, with hugs that literally squeezed the breath out of me. The patio was hopping, though, and Jack didn't have time to stay and chat. "Excuse me just a minute, would you?"

I nodded to people I knew and some who seemed to know me

even though I could have sworn I'd never seen them before in my life. One of these, a large woman in a flowered dress and floppy straw hat, embraced me as if I were her favorite relative. "Lynn!" she said delightedly, so I knew she hadn't mistaken me for Cousin Judy. She took my hands in both of hers and examined my face. "You look as lovely as ever!" A dyke maybe? Turning my palms down, she inspected my left hand.

"No ring yet?" she asked, disappointed.

"No, I guess not," I replied politely.

"Ida, come here!" she called to someone who looked vaguely familiar. I think she was a cousin of Harold's once or twice removed. "Look, no ring yet."

Ida inspected my naked ring finger. Usually I wear a silver band with a pink triangle there, but my hands had been too heat-swollen that morning to put it on.

"What's wrong with that Harold?" Ida said, shaking her head. "He better not let a catch like you get away!"

"Well, you see—"

"Let's give him a talking-to, Fran." At least the floppy-hatted woman had a name now.

Fran and Ida beckoned wildly to Harold, who was standing close by with his mother and a young couple who must have been Cousin Allan and the Rabbi's Daughter. When he couldn't ignore their frantic waves anymore, Harold excused himself and came to join us.

"Ida! Fran!" he said, greeting both of them with a kiss on the cheek.

"Harold, you're a bad boy," Ida scolded. I still had no idea how these people were related to Harold and what interest they had in our being engaged or married. She held up my left hand directly in front of his face. "There's no ring on this finger!"

Harold swallowed hard, and I could sympathize with his predicament. Should he lie further, making everything worse when he came out at the end of the day? Or should he just get it over with now, starting slowly with these distant relatives and working his way up to his parents?

"You know, I've told you before, Cousin Morty can get you a really good deal on a beautiful ring.... Morty, come over here!" Now Ida was motioning to Morty, a short, slightly balding man I remembered meeting once before. Morty became part of the circle. "Morty, tell Harold how you can get him a good deal on something pretty for this girl."

My heart went out to Harold, who looked miserable. Before long the whole extended clan would be discussing our need for an engagement ring and where we could get the best deal.

"Sure, I could set you up with something very nice," Morty said with a wink at me.

Harold looked like he might cry. Suddenly Ruthie, his mother, and Aunt Miriam had joined the discussion with polite smiles at me. "What's going on here? Are you torturing our poor Harold?"

"We noticed," Fran pointed out, "that this darling girl isn't wearing a ring yet, and we're trying to do something about it."

"Now Fran, Ida, Morty," Ruthie said in a clipped tone, looking from one to the other as she said their names, "you know that decision is Harold's and Lynn's. We can't push them into anything."

I started to fantasize that when Harold actually came out, it might be a relief to his mother and aunt. I pictured his mother throwing up her hands with a big smile and saying, "Thank God! Now just find yourself a nice Jewish boy and I can die happy!"

But Harold didn't seem to be having any fantasies, except maybe of escape or mass murder. I tugged gently at his arm. "Harold, I haven't said happy birthday to Bubbe yet. Would you come with me?"

That got us away from the wedding planners, but it was a long trip across the patio and lawn to where Bubbe sat enthroned on a white wicker chair under a canopy. "Thanks for saving me," Harold sighed. "I owe you one."

"You owe me five or six," I said. "But who's counting?"

On our way through the crowd to Bubbe, I was almost bumped into the pool by a fast-moving child, and Harold nearly overturned a waiter's tray of hors d'oeuvres. We were waylaid by Uncle Jack, who told Harold he had a new leather travel kit for him that he should take when he left. "Our latest style," he said proudly. "Very handsome. Soft as a baby's bottom."

And Harold's father, Ben, stopped us to tell us how much our coming meant to Bubbe. "Go say 'happy birthday,' " he urged. "She doesn't think she's going to make it to ninety-one, even though she's like an ox."

"That's what we're trying to do," Harold replied shortly, pulling me behind him by the hand.

Morty had somehow worked his way across the patio before us and called out as we passed, "Don't forget my offer, Harold!"

Bubbe looked great, not a day over eighty-five. Though she was in good health, she couldn't stand for very long or, more likely, didn't want to. If I'm still around at ninety, I'm going to sit every chance I get.

"Bubbe!" Harold said, rushing to hug her. "Happy birthday! Look, Lynn came too. You remember Lynn?"

"Of course I remember Lynn," Bubbe said with a click of her tongue. "How should I not remember Lynn? My body may be old, but my mind is young as ever!" She tapped a finger repeatedly to her temple.

I brushed her soft cheek with my lips. Despite her age, her skin felt and smelled like a baby's. "Happy birthday, Mrs. Fine," I said with a big smile.

She took my hands in both of hers, as she always did. The skin on her hands, in contrast to her face, was like flaky tissue-paper wrapping. Then, to my and Harold's dismay, she turned my palms down just as Ida had. "Vhat, no ring?" she said. I realized that in the time it took us to make our way to Bubbe, Ida and Fran had already worked the crowd with their news about our lack of news.

"It's my ninetieth birthday," Bubbe added sadly, "and you couldn't give me the one thing that vould make me happy — to see my oldest grandson engaged?" She shook her head back and forth dramatically.

"Bubbe—"

"You're thirty-nine years old, Harold," Bubbe observed. "Vhat is it vith you — are you gay?"

The word "gay" rambled across the rolling lawn and hushed the relatives who were standing in court around Bubbe, including Harold's mother. My mouth dropped open, and Harold turned the color of the red roses blooming in Aunt Miriam's garden. He took a deep breath, and his hand squeezed mine for support. "As a matter of fact, Bubbe, I am," he said quickly and loudly with his chin raised. "I've known I was gay for years."

I peeked up, waiting for the skies to open with hail and brimstone, but they remained clear, bright, and sunny. The entire party seemed to be suspended, like someone had pushed the "pause" button.

Everyone looked to Bubbe, who blew her nose into her handkerchief and shifted her focus away from Harold. "Sorry," she said to me with genuine sympathy.

"It's okay," I said, reaching over and patting her papery hand. "I'm gay too."

Afterward we sat in the only diner in town that was open on Sunday, drinking Budweisers and smoking cigarettes. Harold didn't smoke — hadn't smoked a cigarette since he was nineteen, in fact — but decided a few puffs that day couldn't hurt.

"I read somewhere recently," I said, trying to be helpful, "that this is exactly what you should do after you come out."

"Smoke and drink beer?" he said, coughing.

"No, leave and give everyone a little breathing space," I said. I had been only too glad to hightail it out of Aunt Miriam and Uncle Jack's. Whispers had followed us as we made our way from Bubbe's throne to the house and then finally to the safety of Harold's rental car.

"Did you know...?"

"Well, I always thought...."

"What a heartbreak for Ben and Ruthie...."

"Do you think he has...*it*?"

"I'm glad I was with you, Harold," I admitted. "I take back all the miserable, unsupportive things I said to you about tricking me into coming here on Gay Pride Day. I mean, how could we *be* any more proudly gay? We came out to dozens of suburban heterosexuals. They'll talk about this for years. I'm proud of us!"

"But nobody really said good-bye. And Uncle Jack didn't give me the travel kit he said he had for me," Harold said with a sniffle, though I knew he cared only about the snub, not the actual gift.

"Oh, we left in kind of a rush," I noted. "We didn't really say good-bye to them either. And next time I bet Jack has a travel kit *and* a wallet for you." I looked over again at the dessert display, wondering how a piece of apple pie would go with beer. We had never really gotten around to eating at the party, unless you count the two mini-quiches I sneaked on my way over to Bubbe.

"Say, how do you think Bubbe guessed that you're gay?" I asked. "She always seems so old-world to me, like she just got off the boat from...well, wherever she's from. But I guess she's more current than I thought."

"She watches Sally Jessy Raphael every day," Harold explained. "If you ask me, she's got a crush on the woman." He segued into his Bubbe voice: " 'Vhat a talented Jewish girl, vith her own show! And so nice-looking too.' "

I shuddered at the idea of Bubbe or anyone getting all her information about gay people from Sally Jessy. One of the only times I'd seen the show (granted, it was a few years before lesbians became chic), the theme du jour was "Pretty Lesbians" — a clear oxymoron, the host wanted us to believe.

"Hey," I remembered suddenly, "speaking of talk shows, want to hear the other thing I read about coming out?"

"What's that got to do with talk shows?"

"It seems like a topic for a talk show. You know, 'Gay People Who Came Out to Their Parents — The Aftermath'?"

"Okay, since you're such a font of coming-out wisdom, go ahead."

"So, the other thing is that you should do something really gay after you come out to your parents." I glanced at my Tweety Bird watch, and it wasn't even 2 o'clock. "If we blow this pop stand now, we'll still have plenty of time to march in the parade."

94

Harold hesitated — I think he was enjoying his dejection — then asked, "And go to the rally and the fireworks tonight?" in his five-year-old-boy voice.

"Sure."

"And the dance on the pier too?"

I deliberated for a minute on that one. The dance on the pier was a crush of gyrating, sweaty, near-naked men oozing testosterone, and I would have rather gone to the Clit Club for some female energy and bodily fluids. But what if Lexy or Jude were there or, worse, *both* of them?

"Okay, okay," I gave in. "The dance too."

"Oh, Lynnie," Harold said with a grin, reaching across the table toward my hand. I thought we were going to have a tender moment, but he was just grabbing the check. "You're the best lesbian fiancée a boy could ever have!"

Being with Harold for a day and an evening was a refreshing change from the previous week. Harold didn't want anything from me but what he called my "fabulous company." With Lexy and Jude I had begun to feel like I was expected to perform — that if I couldn't "get it up," so to speak, I had some huge sexual problem. Had my sex drive really decreased so drastically over the years?

When I first met Claire, we couldn't get enough of each other. The first few weeks, if I didn't have a couple of orgasms a day, it was unusual. I had been dating Lexy for only a few weeks, and Jude for just one, and already I was feeling cramped and put-upon. Instead of turning me on, the plea of "Fuck me, baby" was starting to make me tired. I wasn't sure if it was age or just plain lack of interest.

When I got home at 1 A.M. from the dance on the pier with blisters from marching and walking and walking and dancing, my answering machine was flashing four red blinks. One hang-up, a message from Lexy ("If you get home early, give me a call, okay?"), a message from Jude ("If you get home early, give me a call, okay?"), and a final hang-up. I knew that 1 in the morning was still early by Lexy's clock, but I wasn't sure about Jude's. Instead of calling either,

I turned off the phone's ringer, tumbled into bed, and slept for nine hours.

In the morning I padded downstairs to get my mail, dressed in the extra-large John Lennon T-shirt I wore when I slept alone and my bright red beach flip-flops, which made a distinctive *slap-slap-slap* sound in the hallway that my neighbors had come to recognize. A door upstairs creaked open, and Jonathan's voice yelled down to me, "Lynn?"

"Hi, Jon. Happy Gay Pride!"

"Oh, happy Gay Pride," he said distractedly, as if he'd forgotten all about it. "Could you stop up here for a minute?"

"Sure." I tugged at my shirt to make sure it covered my butt and flapped my way up to the fourth floor.

Jonathan had left their door ajar for me. The layout of the apartment was a carbon copy of mine except that it was furnished with tasteful country antiques that Jonathan and Alec had bought at tag sales on foraging trips to New Jersey. Instead of institutional white walls, they had painted theirs a rich forest green and stenciled delicate vines in contrasting ivory just below the ceiling.

Often their apartment emanated tantalizing smells — Jonathan was a gourmet cook devoted to Marcella Hazan, and I had enjoyed everything from mushroom lasagna to seafood risotto there — but now it exuded the strong odor of an unidentifiable mixed herb potion. Jonathan and Alec had been consulting a Chinese herbalist who treated AIDS patients. I suddenly panicked that Alec had a new infection.

"Jonathan? Alec?" I called.

Jonathan came out of the kitchen wearing an apron that said CONTROL QUEEN in squeezed and rigid little letters across the chest. "Hey, Lynn," he said with a small smile. His eyes had big black raccoon circles under them. "Nice shirt."

97

"Nice apron. Is everything okay?" I asked, hurrying to get the chitchat out of the way. "Where's Alec?"

"He's resting," Jonathan said. "He ran a high fever last night and had trouble sleeping. I'm just mixing up a witch's brew." I could tell he was trying very hard to be charming in spite of the fact that he felt like shit. He motioned for me to sit down on their elegant mohair couch. "Thanks for coming up. I wanted to ask you a favor."

"Sure. Anything." Because my schedule during the day was more open than most people's, I had taken Alec to doctor and acupuncture appointments on quite a few occasions while Jonathan went to work. The last time Alec came home from a hospital stay, I had waited with him for an hour every morning until the home-care worker arrived.

"Alec and I rented a cottage in Cherry Grove for a week, starting this coming Friday," Jonathan continued. "We reserved it last summer, optimistically, I guess, and now I don't think we should go. His fever's been up and down all week — well, you don't need all the gory details — and we both think it's not a great time to travel, even though the ocean and sun might be good for him. I don't like the idea of being so far away from his doctor. I was wondering if you'd like to use the cottage for the week so it doesn't go to waste? You've been such a sweetheart to us, and I thought maybe you could use it to write."

The words "Cherry Grove" had dropped me down in the middle of a fantasy — a cozy blue clapboard cottage right on the ocean, gently lapping waves seducing me to sleep every night, a Pulitzer-caliber play practically writing itself, gorgeous women in bikinis and maillots at a comfortable distance....

But I couldn't take the vacation gratis. I knew they had

undoubtedly saved for months from Jonathan's modest teaching salary to buy such a prime week on Fire Island, which included the Fourth of July. Alec had been a public-school teacher too but had been on disability since the first of the year. "You're very sweet," I said, sincerely touched by the offer, "and I'd love to go, but only if I can pay for it."

We haggled for a few minutes, Jonathan maintaining that I should accept the week for free, me determined to reimburse them. Exhausted and probably just wanting to get rid of me so he could finish his herb concoction, Jonathan finally saw it my way. I told him that I would take Harold, who could afford to pay for half the rent. "You dykes drive a hard bargain," Jonathan said. "Alec will be delighted that you're going in our place."

"I think I'll just run downstairs right now and start packing," I said, not because I really needed five days to cram some T-shirts and cutoffs into a suitcase but because it was such a hard, mixed moment — happy for me and sad for them at the same time — and neither of us seemed to feel free enough to express our emotions. "I'm not even sure I have a bathing suit, it's been such a long time since I went to the beach."

"Yeah, it would be embarrassing to wear a little skirted one."

"Hey, I hear those are coming back," I said, punching him playfully in the arm. I'm not sure who initiated it, but the punch somehow metamorphosed into a hug.

My employer wasn't very happy about my decision to spend a week at the beach.

"But when will you have the final outline ready for me?" April demanded on the phone. Uncharacteristically, she had called me up herself instead of asking Jude to do it for her. I had already missed one deadline for the outline, and now I was going on vacation.

"That's what I'll be working on at the beach," I lied. I had no intention of ruining a vacation at a gay beach resort worrying about the biological differences between men and women. I had started the outline for April's book more than once from her notes, but all I could think of was *Who cares?* "I have a modem right in my laptop, so I can just fax it over to you." What kind of hole was I digging for myself? About three by six, it seemed.

"As soon as you come back, then, I want to have another meeting," she insisted. "I've had some thoughts about lesbians."

"Oh?" I said casually, thinking, *I'll bet you have.*

"About incorporating them into the book, the way you've been suggesting," she finished.

"That's great!" I always held a cockeyed optimist's hope that straight feminists like April would finally "get it," would wake up one morning and understand what lesbian oppression had to do with them. "Will you have Jude set up the time?"

"Hmm," she said vaguely. "Jude. I've had some thoughts about Jude too."

"Is anything wrong?"

"Well, she's been so strange the past week, acting scattered and disorganized, like she's off in another world. I hope I didn't make a mistake hiring her. But I can't just let her go, you see. I mean, Jill *Womann*..."

So if Jude hadn't been Jill Womann's daughter, April might have thrown her out on her ear without so much as a warning. I gritted my teeth. "Maybe you should let her know there's a problem," I suggested. "Try to figure out a solution together. That way, if you eventually do have to let her go, it won't be a total surprise."

"Yes, yes, that's a good idea," April agreed. "Lynn, dear, I can always depend on you to be so clear and levelheaded!"

It was my turn to say "Hmm."

I considered just disappearing, not letting anyone else know where I'd be for one whole week. Harold would be with me, Jonathan and Alec knew where I was, April had the number — did I have any obligation to tell anyone else? My friendship with Beth had soured over the past few weeks, and I realized that when it came down to it, she was primarily Claire's friend. The last time I had spoken to her was just before the infamous mediation session.

"Claire's really got high hopes for this meeting," Beth had related. I resented it that she had taken it on herself to prime me for Claire's expectations. Did she care what my thoughts and feelings about being summoned to mediation were?

"High hopes for what?" I asked, and my tone may have been just a little bit snippy.

"You don't have to get nasty," Beth said. "High hopes that you'll be able to talk about what happened between the two of you...to be friends again."

"I told her when she left, I don't want to be friends," I reminded Beth. "I hate that whole lesbian shtick — you and your new lover are best friends with your ex-lover and her new lover, and the two new lovers used to be lovers, and now everybody is one big happy 'family of choice.' I don't believe for a minute that there isn't hideous leftover relationship shit that comes out later. Nobody's *that* mature."

"You're such a cynic."

"Maybe I am," I admitted. "But tell me, how many of your old boyfriends do you and Paul chum around with now, hmm?"

I thought that would stop her in her tracks, but she had one good parting shot. "And since when do *you* follow the example of straight people?" Beth asked.

I hadn't spoken to Beth since. In my own paranoid way, I began to suspect that everything I said to her went right to Claire in a direct current. And though it might be satisfying to know that Claire knew I was enjoying myself in Cherry Grove, it was just as satisfying to have her know nothing about my life at all.

Then, of course, there was the question of Jude and Lexy. Jude already knew, because April had informed her when she asked her to set up a meeting, and Jude called, very businesslike and official. Not at all like the sweet messages she'd been leaving on my answering machine for the last two days: "Did you survive your family party?"; "Hey, can I buy you lunch sometime soon?"

When she phoned on April's behalf, she actually said, "This is Jude Mann."

"Jude Mann?" I joked. "Not *the* Jude Mann!" When there wasn't any giggling at the other end, I took the offensive. "Since when do you have to tell your paramour your last name?"

"Is that what you are — my paramour?" she said in a clipped tone. "Doesn't that have lurid overtones?"

"No, they're definitely undertones. So do you want to tell me what this undertone of *yours* is about?" It was Tuesday, and I hadn't returned her messages from Sunday or Monday afternoon. I had a pretty good idea what the undertone was about.

"Well, I called you Sunday and Monday, and you didn't bother to call back," she said crisply. "I left two messages for you." Then, with less confidence and probably because she realized she was bordering on obsession, she added, "Did you get them?"

102

"I did. I've just been swamped," I lied. I'd mostly been talking to Harold on the phone, planning our vacation week. "I was going to return phone calls tonight. Hey, did April mention that I'm spending next week at the beach?" I thought I'd toss it into the conversation casually, to make it sound like no big deal.

"Yes, of course she did," she replied in an icy tone. "That's great for you."

"Yeah. I haven't had a vacation in a year," I said, memories of the last vacation with Claire in San Diego flooding back. We'd visited old friends of ours, and for most of the trip, Claire was distant and uncommunicative with me but not with them. Finally, tired of being ignored, I treated us to a deluxe night at the Hotel del Coronado, the nineteenth-century resort just across the bridge from San Diego. "We always stay with friends; we haven't had a real hotel vacation in years," I pointed out as I plunked down my Gold Card.

Restored to its Victorian splendor, the hotel was like a fairyland, all wondrous wooden cupolas and spires with a maze of staircases and passageways connecting the various wings. I got lost a couple of times just going to get ice. One of the first Otis cage elevators ever built still operated in the main lobby, and we rode it up and down half a dozen times like kids, even though it didn't lead to our wing. We played *Some Like It Hot*, which was filmed at the hotel in the '50s, Claire pretending to be Marilyn Monroe to my Tony Curtis. Our room was not luxurious — no fireplace; I didn't spring for that, but then, who needs one in San Diego in late July? — but it was crisp and quaint with a comfortable queen-size bed that we had spectacular sex in.

Claire looked happy and animated for the twenty-some hours we were there, and since she'd been moody for the whole beginning of the trip, I figured the atmosphere at the Coronado — or "the Del," as the staff calls it — was well worth the expense. Whatever had been bothering Claire seemed to vanish with the ghosts of the old hotel. When we broke up she told me that night was the last time I had really paid attention to her.

Of course, I didn't say any of this to Jude.

"You'll have a whole house to yourself?" Jude was asking, fishing for an invitation.

"No, Harold will be there too," I said, not taking the bait, determined to have a week without pressures. "You remember Harold? The Garden Party? Freda Chews?"

"Sure, sure," she said, but I could tell her thoughts were elsewhere. "Well, that sounds great."

"I'm sorry, but I'm really busy this week," I said. I was a monster, and I couldn't seem to help it. "Could we make plans for the week I get back?"

There was a long stretch of nothing; then, "Just tell me now," she said in a very low voice, maybe so April couldn't hear. "Is *she* going with you? Are you breaking up with me?"

"I told you, it's just me and Harold. And I'd love to see you when I get back," I assured her, not really answering the question because it seemed so silly. How do you "break up" after a handful of dates? "But Jude, this is a casual thing, remember? You said so yourself."

"Right," she agreed with just a whisper of hesitation. "Yes, of course, you're right. Could we start over? I'm being stupid."

"No, you're not. Let's just make a date, all right?"

One down, one to go.

Lexy had a couple of weeks' dating seniority on Jude, so she seemed to feel perfectly justified in making demands. "I've got a great idea! I could take Tuesday off and spend a long weekend with you. I've only been to Cherry Grove once before."

"It's a tiny cottage, Lexy, and, well...Harold's coming, and—"

"Oh, I've wanted to meet him — he sounds really cool," she enthused. "We could, like, hang out and get to know each other. Is he bringing his drag?"

"No, that's just for performances; he doesn't wear it around," I said impatiently. I got tired of people assuming that drag queens go to the office in high heels and lipstick. "Anyway, I think Harold would be uncomfortable with that setup — you and me and him," I added, though, in fact, Harold would undoubtedly be highly amused by the whole thing. "He's been single for a long time, and you and I are kind of loud when we have sex, and—"

"Oh, is that all?" she said, laughing. "Well, we'll just have to fuck *very quietly*." Her voice dropped to a lascivious hush.

"No, really, I'm serious. Harold will feel left out," I insisted. "You and I could take a trip together some other time. Okay?"

Nothing, not even a breath.

"Lexy? Okay?"

"Is *she* going with you? Is that it?" she asked impatiently. "Are you taking the debutante?"

"First of all," I said sternly, "it's just me and Harold, like I said." I was about to add "I don't lie," but she already knew that wasn't true. "Second, 'the debutante' is just the assistant to the woman I'm working for right now."

"What's her name?" she persisted.

"What is this all about, Lexy?" I asked, getting really tired of the inquisition.

"I don't know," she said with a deep sigh, and I believed her.

"Thinking about you dating that…that Smith girl or whatever she is is just kind of upsetting."

I almost corrected her by saying "Vassar," but luckily I stopped myself just in time.

Lexy was out of control, and I was convinced this whatever-it-was we were immersed in was heading straight for a brick wall. But she wasn't being as out of touch as I'm making her sound. We had spent an inordinate amount of time together during the first few weeks of our affair, throwing it into overdrive. By now a lot of lesbian couples I knew would have moved in together or been well on their way to it. Claire and I had shacked up after eight weeks. There's that tired old joke that seems like a stereotype but is truer than you think: "What does a lesbian bring on the second date? A U-Haul." Though Lexy and I both intended to be casual when we started off, feelings and jealousies have a habit of getting in the way. And the truth is, if it had been the other way around, I know I would have felt hideously jealous.

Still, though I knew all of this, I held fast to my plan to recuperate and regroup for a week with Harold. In the end I relented only enough to give Lexy the phone number of the cottage on the island. Was that my fatal mistake? Did that convince her she had certain rights?

When I look back now, I wonder what would have happened if I had just disappeared after all.

"This," Harold said with a lazy smile, "is definitely the life."

We rented low-slung beach chairs and a gaudy rainbow beach umbrella and parked ourselves near the foamy waves with mystery novels and a thermos of cranberry iced tea. Harold and I took turns slathering each other with SPF 30 and watching out for babes of either sex. Occasionally I'd catch Harold glancing down at his stomach in exactly the same way that I did to make sure it wasn't sagging, though he didn't have any flab to speak of.

"Babe Alert, Babe Alert," Harold would say out of the corner of his mouth, and it might be a Clit Clubber carrying the top half of her string bikini in her hand or a Chelsea Gym boy with fabulous tits ambling by our chairs. Whichever gender, we would both watch the show appreciatively from over our books, trying to keep track of the twisting mystery plots in between sightings. I was reading an engrossing lesbian mystery that had so many characters, I had to keep referring to the "Cast of Characters" at the front of the book for help, since I lost my bearings every time the Babe Alert siren went off.

This went on for a couple of days of easy and oblivious bliss.

Babe sighting became a job that we took very seriously, only running back to the cottage to pee or to grab something to eat. Of course, neither of us would have dreamed of approaching any of the elusive creatures we spotted, though we talked about it incessantly — "Maybe I should just walk up to her; she's alone right now" or "God, can you imagine what it must be like to *do* him?" But then we'd readjust our sunglasses and settle back into our mystery plots, enjoying our role as voyeurs of life.

At 6 or 6:30, just like office commuters in Manhattan, we'd pack up our provisions and head back to the cottage for cocktails. My fantasy of a place right on the beach was, in fact, pure fantasy. Miniature studios overlooking the beach could run over a thousand bucks a week in high season, so our more affordable two-bedroom quarters were right smack in the middle of Cherry Grove in a particularly tropical and claustrophobic enclave.

"Probably one of the oldest cottages still standing in the Grove. Goes all the way back to the '30s," the real estate agent told us proudly when she handed over the key. That, we discovered, was just another way to say "ramshackle." The entrance path was overrun with out-of-control foliage, and we had to fight our way to the house. The screen door was coming off its hinges, and the sliding screen entry onto the deck had a gash in it that killer mosquitoes seemed to regard as their private entrance. The deck sat almost right on the boardwalk, and passersby could gawk at us as we slouched there like animals in the zoo, lapping up our evening gin and tonics. All the furniture inside was either molded plastic or scratchy synthetic, and the bedsprings on our narrow beds moaned with every little movement. In the torrid July heat, the whole house had only one small fan — probably from the 1930s too — which clacked and sputtered and gasped out an ineffectual wheeze. We tried not to think about how much we were shelling out for this luxurious habitat.

The place had its own charm, though, which mostly came from our imaginations. We envisioned W.H. Auden crashing there with friends during one of his summers in the Grove, when the house was relatively new. Harold even began to play the poet's role, affecting a passable British accent.

"Darling, can I bring you anything?"

"Yes, Wystan, could you fetch another G and T?" I called from the deck. I don't know who I was pretending to be, but with the amount of gin I was consuming, I could have been Carson McCullers. Years before, I had read a biography of her, and a photo of Carson at the writers colony at Yaddo, carrying around a thermos of spiked tea, had stuck in my mind.

"It's like time is on vacation too," Harold observed, plopping down next to me with a refill for both of us. "You know your theory about how time is speeding up the older we get? Well, here I feel like time is in a holding pattern, like maybe we'll wake up tomorrow and be fifteen years younger. I haven't seen anyone who looks sick. I'm telling you, it's like Cherry Grove is in a time warp."

I didn't want to say, *You're seeing what you want to see,* but I thought that was what was going on. Harold knew as well as I that people with HIV needed to avoid direct sunlight or wear a very high-number sunscreen, so many avoided idling on the beach all day. The epidemic was here too; you could feel it lurking — it just wasn't visible on the scorching sands, where we'd been spending most waking hours.

I could have gone on this way for weeks, months maybe, forgetting Lexy and Jude and April and Claire and everything that pushed and tugged at me in the city. As housemates, Harold and I got along pretty well, considering that we'd never lived together and both had idiosyncrasies that we immediately learned about. The first night I watched Harold set up a gadget in his room that he'd carted from the city. It looked a little like an answering machine, but since there was no phone in his bedroom, I knew that couldn't be right.

"What's that thing?" I asked.

"An environmental sound machine," he replied, jabbing a button on a complicated display panel. "Listen to this!" The machine replicated the sounds of the ocean's surf, overlaid with faint, distant cries of seagulls and the occasional tinkle of a buoy bell. "Doesn't it sound real?"

"Yeah, totally. Except that if you turned it off, you'd probably hear the same thing. We're *at* the beach, Harold."

"I used to have incredible insomnia, and this machine cured me," he said. "I can't sleep without it." He pushed some other buttons to demonstrate the machine's amazing capability to sound just like a rainstorm, a waterfall, or a babbling brook. Since I was someone who was dead to the world minutes after my head hit the pillow, it was hard for me to appreciate the device.

I also learned that Harold's morning ritual included monopolizing *The New York Times* while drinking cup after cup of coffee and eating, in courses, what to me seemed like enormous amounts of food: first, Special K with bananas, then a bran muffin or two, a bowl of fresh blueberries and vanilla yogurt, finally ending with Entenmann's raspberry swirl coffee cake — dessert, I guess.

"I'm amazed you can still eat like that and stay thin," I observed as I picked at my single slice of whole wheat toast. "You eat like a teenage boy."

"Everything I ate is low-fat — well, except this coffee cake. Anyway, breakfast and lunch should be your biggest meals," he remarked, licking icing from his finger. "That way you work off the calories during the day." It sounded like good advice, but I'd never noticed that he skimped at dinner.

"We don't work off dick out here," I noted. "All we do here is sit on our butts on the beach."

"Babe watching takes a lot out of you. It requires energy to stay alert and on top of the situation." He said it with a straight face, but when he ducked behind the paper's business section, I saw a hint of a smile.

"Well, could you stop being so 'on top of' the *Times* and hand over the front page?"

Harold learned things about me too. "What do you do in there for such a long time?" he asked me the second morning, when I took my habitual forty-five minutes in the bathroom. "It takes me fifteen minutes tops. And *I* have to shave."

"The usual stuff," I said, seeing no need to outline my ritual for him, since it included a full twenty-five minutes of reading magazines on the can. *People* was my favorite, but a copy of *Out*, the lesbian and gay high-gloss magazine, would do in a pinch. Both told me all about what Ellen, k.d., Melissa, and Martina were up to. If I felt rushed or didn't get the time I needed, the day was shot, and I was a bitch. "Look, Harold, you don't want to *know* me if I don't get my full time in the bathroom." He wrinkled his nose and gave up.

Then there was my tendency to leave dirty dishes in the sink for days without being bothered in the least. After two days of that, Harold asked for some house rules, notably, "Dishes won't be left in the sink for longer than twenty-four hours," which I agreed to, then promptly forgot. Who can remember when the 24-hour period started anyway?

111

But there wasn't much time to get bugged by each other's peculiarities, since pretty soon Harold was getting laid, and I was starring in my very own soap opera.

On Sunday we made friends with the people in the bungalow next to ours, a lesbian couple and a single gay man. Actually, the way we became acquainted was that the man cruised Harold on the beach — nothing too serious, just a big smile and a "Hey, there" kind of look — and then spotted us out on our deck on his way to the grocery store.

"Hey," he said, "didn't I see you on the beach?" He meant Harold, but he looked back and forth at both of us. "Under that big rainbow umbrella?"

"Yep, that's us," I said when Harold's tongue seemed to be tied. "I'm Lynn, and this is Harold." His name was Carl, and he was very handsome, with a body chiseled out of smooth mahogany, enviably high cheekbones, and shoulder-length dreds. I nudged Harold, trying to get him to speak, but he merely smiled and sipped his drink nervously. Harold has always been very self-conscious about his looks, though he is perfectly adorable, small-boned but not scrawny, with a mop of reddish-brown curls that are always falling into his eyes.

"I wish I were buff," Harold had sighed that afternoon after Carl tried to flirt with him on the beach. "Maybe I should go to the gym. There's one in the Pines." Eying some perfectly sculpted men splashing in the water right in front of us, Harold looked as if he wanted to find a quick fix of muscles, an overnight transformation of his delicate frame.

But Carl seemed to like Harold just the way he was. At any rate he didn't waste a minute inviting us over. "Looks like I'm right next door to you," Carl observed, nodding toward a cute shell-pink cottage tucked away in a sanctuary of trees. It had a homemade wooden sign nailed to the fence in front of it with the name HOMO HAVEN painted in lavender. "My housemates and I are having some folks over to the Haven for a Third of July barbecue. We're not into all the patriotism shit that happens on the Fourth, y'know? So anyway, there'll be plenty of food, nice people. Wanna come?"

"Sure," I said, accepting for both of us. "That would be great. Wouldn't that be great, Harold?" I knew if I didn't drag him into the conversation, he'd sit comatose through the whole thing.

"Yeah," Harold finally offered, proving he had a voice. "That would be great."

"Great," Carl said, obviously a little nervous himself. "Anytime after 8. I'll see *you* then." His index finger pointed playfully at Harold, who smiled shyly and gulped his cocktail as Carl disappeared down the path.

"What the fuck is wrong with you?" I burst out, even though I knew it wouldn't help the situation.

"There's nothing wrong with me," Harold said, visibly hurt.

"Okay, okay, there's nothing wrong with you," I agreed, softening my tone. "But Harold, for God's sake, he's such a cute boy, and he *likes* you."

"You think?" Harold asked in his kid voice.

"Yes, I think. I *know*. He was cruising you like crazy."

"Should we, I don't know, like, go to the party?" he ventured. Harold's uncharacteristic slip into Lexy language made her face suddenly visualize in my mind. Was it possible that I missed her?

"Of course we should go to the party!" I said, jumping up and dissolving the image of Lexy. "And you, Harold Fine, are going to do me a favor. Face it, you owe me about a dozen after Chappaqua. Here's all I want — I want you to try to remember for one evening, *please,* what a cute, funny, exceptional person you are."

"You think?" He rattled the ice cubes in his glass with a bashful grin that suggested he was just beginning to believe me.

That night I met some interesting people whom I wanted to keep in touch with in the city, including Carl's lesbian housemates, Colleen and Eve. Colleen had obviously been born fair-haired — she had pale skin and a smattering of freckles — but had recently dyed her hair a severe blackish brown. She had tired of people staring at her and Eve not only as a lesbian couple but as an interracial one at that and felt dark hair drew less attention than her natural strawberry blond. Eve had supported her lover's decision and even helped her apply the Nice 'n Easy a couple of weeks before. "Believe me," Eve quipped, "it's not so easy."

At the party Colleen entertained us with fascinating psychological-behavior anecdotes — a sort of compendium of before-and-after stories — about strangers' and casual acquaintances' being more respectful of her as a brunet than as a blond, assuming intelligence instead of flightiness.

"So blonds don't really have more fun after all," I kidded, but Colleen looked like she was in her late twenties and a little too young for the 1960s hair-color commercial reference. Eve, who seemed to be about my age, got the joke immediately.

"But we all sure believed that they did!" she remarked. "My older sister bleached her hair when she was in high school. Oh, the good old days."

I was dying to ask her, how does age come into your relationship?

— but it was too intense a question for the party, and besides, it seemed a little personal to ask someone I'd just met. What if age was a very big deal for them? Or what if they were really closer in age than they looked?

About 1 A.M. I left Harold at the barbecue, deep in a conversation with Carl about the best restaurants in Manhattan, and wandered back to the cottage alone. "You go home. He'll be fine," Eve assured me when I showed some weird maternal reluctance to leave him, even though I was tired. "They're really hitting it off."

"He just hasn't dated in a really long time," I said with one more protective glance back at him.

"All the more reason for him to get to it," she said with a gentle push on my back. "Go home, Mom."

I guess I don't have to tell you that that night, Harold didn't need his environmental sound machine.

Fourth of July, I had forgotten, is a drag holiday on the island. Harold had apparently forgotten it too, since he hadn't brought Freda Chews's wardrobe with him, which required its own suitcase. The afternoon of July 4, gaily costumed drag queens from Cherry Grove depart en masse in boats to take a ten-minute sail up the bay to Fire Island Pines, the Grove's sister community, where they are greeted by a swarm of queens, just as wildly decked out. The whole thing lasts a couple of hours and is called the Invasion. It's been taking place for about twenty years.

I realized I was going to be right in the middle of the embarkation when I went to buy the *Times* that morning on the pier. "You here for the Invasion?" a gray-haired man behind me on line for the paper asked.

"No, actually, I forgot all about it. It's today, right?"

"Oh, yes," he said earnestly. "I haven't missed an Invasion since the first one. What an exciting time *that* was! Not that long after Stonewall, and all of us bursting out of the closet! And before the plague.... Well, I haven't been able to tolerate the heat lately, so I'm not actually in the middle of things anymore, but..." He drew out a worn wallet. "...that was me then!" he finished proudly, producing a color snapshot.

He had been a stunning Carol Channing in full Dolly Levi attire — tight red gown and matching parasol with a feathery tiara atop a platinum blond wig — stepping ladylike into a water taxi. "Well, well, hell-o, Lou-is," he started crooning in her voice. Then he pocketed the picture. "Bet you'd never guess it looking at me now!" He did seem much shorter, though it was probably just because he wasn't wearing spiked heels. But there was a sparkle somewhere in his eyes that suggested high camp.

"Oh, it sounds like you can still do a mean Carol Channing," I winked.

"If it weren't for the heat...." He fanned himself with a folding Chinese fan while we waited our turn on line.

"Yeah, it gets to me too," I agreed. As I plunked down my money for the paper, I thanked him for showing me the photograph and wished him a happy Invasion.

The Invasion meant both the Grove and the Pines would be unusually crowded, since visitors came in for the day just to witness it. The spectacle would be mobbed, and it looked as if I'd have to go it alone, since Harold had shown no signs of returning from his date. I teetered between being happy for him and missing his morning voice calling, "Lynnie! Coffee!" when the pot had brewed.

I decided to treat myself to breakfast at a restaurant near the pier, where I could sit outside and watch the Invasion preparations while I perused the paper. The nice part of Harold's not coming home was that I didn't have to fight him for the crossword puzzle. I opened to the puzzle — which, I have to admit, I've come close to finishing only once in fifteen years, and that was with major assistance from four reference works — found a pen in my pocket, and got to work.

It was the last thing that I expected, but it happened anyway.

"Hey, babe," a familiar voice said, but I ignored it because everyone calls everyone "babe" in the Grove — or seems to.

"Earth to Lynn," the voice said again, and I stopped in the middle of pondering 97-across, a six-letter word for burial markers, and glanced up.

"You must be really good at that to do it in pen." Lexy was leaning on the railing of the restaurant's deck, smiling at me from behind what she herself would call "really cool shades." She was wearing next to nothing — a tight, ribbed, white tank top and a pair of short-short denim cutoffs that exposed her smooth, strong thighs. "I wondered if I'd run into you. Surprised to see me?"

"Well, yeah, sort of. Yeah," I said more definitively. My eyes fell on the leather knapsack slung over her shoulder, the one she used to transport her sex-toy collection back and forth from my apartment. I blushed at the thought.

"My friend Desi asked me out for the Invasion. Her friend Pedro is into drag, and we're staying with him. Hey, Desi, come here a minute." She waved to a tall, handsome woman, who had an arresting tattoo on her upper arm of a black cat arching its back. When I looked more closely, I could see that the cat was formed from the letters of the name "Desiderata."

"Desi Mendez, Lynn Woods," Lexy introduced us casually, and, sitting there wearing my reading glasses and poring over the cross-word puzzle, I suddenly felt like Lexy's dyke aunt.

"Great tattoo," I commented, unable to take my eyes off of it.

"The same guy who did mine," Lexy pointed out. "You should get one, Lynn. It'd look great."

"Mention my name and he'll give you a deal," Desi offered. I sensed that she was sizing me up as competition, then deciding I wasn't any at all. I plucked my glasses off my nose and glanced down at my clothes, a Michigan Womyn's Music Festival T-shirt from 1982, baggy khaki shorts, and flip-flops — my favorite summer weekend outfit. Well, in my defense, I hadn't expected to see anyone I knew on my way to get the paper. Not only did I feel like a dyke aunt but I realized that I looked the part.

"We've got to check in with Pedro, see how his toilette is going," Lexy said breezily. "You gonna be around? Where are you staying?"

"I'm here for the week," I said. I wasn't sure what was called for in this sort of situation, so I ripped off a corner of the crossword puzzle page and scribbled the address.

"Well, we're taking the late boat back tomorrow night so we can both go to work Wednesday, but maybe I'll stop by tomorrow." Lexy pecked me on the cheek like a good niece. I tried not to watch them go off up the path laughing and nudging each other, but I couldn't help it: Lexy looked too good from behind. And I couldn't fight off the pangs of jealousy that were stinging me. Now that it seemed like Harold might have disappeared for the duration, I was cursing myself for not inviting one of my oh-so-willing girlfriends along for company. What kind of idiot was I?

I replaced my glasses, filled in "stelae" in 97-across, and ordered waffles with strawberries, whipped cream, and a side order of bacon. I'm just the opposite of people who lose weight when they're depressed: Loneliness makes me hungry. How soon, I wondered, before I filled out my baggy shorts?

Barbra, Marilyn, Billie, and Judy were tottering to the pier for the launch when I headed back to the cottage with a full stomach, wondering what I was going to do with my day. If Harold stayed with Carl, it was going to be a lot less fun babe watching on the beach. Babe watching with two is a game; with one it's just pathetic. I considered inviting Colleen and Eve, but there were no stirrings of life at Homo Haven when I walked by. When I left at 1 A.M. the party had been in full swing, so it looked as if the residents of the Haven would be dead to the world for a while.

Even though I'd had three or four cups of coffee at the restaurant, I made a full pot and finished reading the paper. In the distance I could hear horns tooting and people cheering as the Invasion began. I tried to do more of the crossword puzzle, but my hand was visibly shaking from the amount of caffeine I'd had. I smoked a handful of cigarettes on the deck, looking wistfully toward the Haven. Still no life.

"Snap out of it!" I said to myself and crushed my cigarette. "You came here to have fun — now go do it!" Gathering up my beach chair, umbrella, and reading material, I took the bold step of going to the beach by myself.

This may not seem like a big deal to you, but gay Fire Island is a social place. You rarely see anyone alone on the beach unless his or her friends have just gone to get more chips or run to the bathroom or are taking a dip in the ocean. The only time I ever saw a man alone, he was sleeping naked with a straw hat over his face, his penis rising tentatively in an erection. This was years ago with Claire, and

I found myself unable to take my eyes off him.

"That man's getting a hard-on," I said to Claire, pointing.

"Yeah? And do you have to watch him do it?"

"No, it's just—"

"Come on, Lynn, are you trying to tell me you've never seen a man get an erection before?" She was right, of course, but wrong too. It wasn't the point that he *could* get an erection or that I particularly wanted to witness it but that he felt free enough to do it right there in front of everyone on the beach.

I couldn't make her understand, so I gave up. But for some reason I remembered it vividly when I plopped down on the sand by myself.

I was just trying to smear my SPF 30 on evenly when, to my great relief, I heard Harold's distinctive voice being lifted over the sand.

"Lynnie, where have you been?"

He was running toward me lightly with a big smile of contentment across his face. I hadn't seen Harold so animated in years. He was slightly out of breath when he reached my chair.

"I looked for you at the pier, but you weren't there," he said. "Carl and Colleen and Eve and I have been waiting for you for the *longest* time!" He pointed down the beach about twenty yards, where the Homo Haven crowd was situated on a big, faded blue quilt. Carl was standing and waving at me. There was someone else on the blanket that I didn't recognize at such a distance, but it seemed to be a young white boy wearing a baseball cap. "I was just about to call out a search party!"

"I thought you were all sleeping," I explained. "I went to the pier early, then stayed at the house for a while. I never thought you'd be up yet."

Harold was already scooping up my beach paraphernalia and lugging it toward their spot. "You look happy," I said with a smile. "Happy," though, wasn't really accurate. Strange as it sounds for a writer, I often find myself at a loss for the right word, the one that hasn't been used to excess until it's become meaningless. Words like "happy" and "nice" and "sweet" pop out of my mouth constantly. I was searching through my mental thesaurus for a better term; something like "enraptured" or "exhilarated" probably would do the trick.

"I'm a new man," he said, and I knew he was being serious. "I'll tell you all about it later. But guess what?" He turned to me with an even more delighted face, one that said he had some really good dish. "You'll never guess who's here!"

"Oh, yeah," I said, dismissing the news indifferently, "I know. I ran into her at the pier. With Deli or Desi or whatever her 'friend's' name is."

He looked at me like I had just started talking to him in Esperanto, his forehead wrinkling and his eyes tapering to slits. "What are you talking about?" he asked.

"Lexy," I said. "I know she's here. I saw her at the pier."

"Lexy's here?" he said with amusement. His face sparkled like a holiday firecracker. "Oh, that's rich. I *love* this." I waited for him to spill the rest of his news, but he held it in until it looked like it might seep out through his nose or ears.

"Fasten your seat belts," he grinned. "It's going to be a bumpy night!"

A spinning in my stomach told me I already knew who the mystery guest was. We reached the Haven's blanket, and there, chatting with our new friends, was Jude.

"I can explain what I'm doing here," Jude whispered as she popped up to kiss my surprised face.

"Okay," I said. "I'm listening." Having Lexy and Jude show up in Cherry Grove when I knew they had both been dying to come with me seemed too much of a coincidence. Even if I had been privately bemoaning the fact that I hadn't invited one or the other along for company, I didn't like the idea of being followed by them, which my paranoid mind was starting to be convinced of. I'd read about people who are stalked by lovers and rejected lovers and unrequited lovers — and, yes, I thought about my own behavior with Claire — and I knew immediately that I was in over my head.

"April and I tried to fax you some notes but couldn't get through," Jude explained. "Actually, what happened is, April called me at home Sunday, begging me to come over and help her. You know, she works all the time and thinks that everybody does. That's the big problem with being her assistant. No boundaries. Anyway, she thought she just couldn't operate the fax machine on her own. She's hopeless with office equipment. So I went over and tried but no luck. Well, April worked herself into a frenzy. She was convinced you just skipped town and weren't working on the outline at all. She told me to get on a train, and here I am."

I shook my head in disbelief. But I didn't bother to tell her that April's guess was right — I *had* brought my computer, but it was at the cottage, in its bag, totally unplugged.

"Honest," Jude said with a worried look. "Cross my heart. I couldn't tell her we were dating and arriving on your doorstep wasn't such a good idea. It was either this or my job."

Knowing April, this was undoubtedly the truth. But knowing Jude, I was sure there were other reasons she hadn't protested April's decree.

My annoyance lasted only a few minutes. There's a certain atmosphere at the Fire Island gay resorts. In the Pines, where there is a majority of gay men, I'm sure it's tangible testosterone, because it feels alien and seductive all at the same time. But in Cherry Grove, where gay women and men mix freely and in more equal numbers, it's something slightly different — a charged feeling of queer sexuality, an ambience of gaiety. I had been thinking about sex for days and masturbating my little fingers off. I felt relieved at the prospect of getting laid.

"It's no problem, really," I reassured Jude, who looked terrified at what I might say or do.

But Harold was at the beach, the house was empty, and I had totally different fish to fry. "Want to see the cottage?" I suggested coyly.

The door to the cottage was a few inches ajar when we made our way up the path, Jude nibbling at my neck all the way and sending delightful shivers through me. When I noticed the door, I had to ask her to stop for a minute, which she did with some reluctance. Harold and I left the front door unlocked when we went to the beach so we didn't have to worry about losing the keys. Everyone did that in the Grove and the Pines — it was a ritualized shedding of the deadbolts, police locks, and fear that ruled our lives in the city, a kind of implicit, though naive, trust that gay people weren't going to rip each other off.

But I knew I hadn't left the door open. Unless it had blown open, someone had been in the house.

Nothing seemed to be amiss in the living room, and the kitchen and my bedroom looked okay, too. My computer was safely in its case. The first thing I checked for in Harold's room was the environmental sound machine, which was still plugged in by the side of the bed. No one had taken his wallet either, which he had left out in full view on the dresser next to a small mound of change. "Harold," I clucked, shoving it into a drawer. I turned around and jumped a couple of feet.

"Jude!" I squealed. She was standing silently in the doorway, watching me double-check everything.

"Sorry, I didn't mean to scare you," she said. "Anything missing?"

"Not that I can tell," I replied.

"Maybe you just didn't pull the door all the way closed when you left," Jude suggested. "It's a pretty flimsy door."

"Yeah, that's probably it," I muttered, but I was unconvinced. My paranoia started working overtime. There was a feeling in the house that someone had been there — nothing tangible, just an essence of intrusion. If I hadn't seen with my own eyes that she was preoccupied with Desi, I would have guessed that it was Lexy. I wasn't sure if I should divulge these fears to Jude or just let her start nibbling on me again. But if I didn't tell her and Lexy showed up, there was bound to be hell to pay.

"When are you going back?" I asked in what was to her an abrupt non sequitur but to me a perfectly sensible question. If she were going back early, we probably wouldn't run into Lexy at all and I wouldn't have to disclose that my other lover was only yards away at the hotel.

"Gee, thanks," Jude said, taking a step back and looking like I'd just told her she had bad breath. "I just got here. I know I wasn't invited, but you seemed to be okay with it, and now—"

"No, no, I just was trying to figure out how much time we have together," I said, smoothly covering my faux pas.

Jude smiled. "Sometime tomorrow morning," she said, coming closer again. "We have all day…and night." She put her arms around my neck and started munching at the nape of my neck. "Oh, wait a sec…."

From her canvas overnight bag she fished a manila envelope with my name on it. It looked fat and imposing. April Ronsard's personal logo — a dainty white hand with a lace cuff holding a pen and drawing a woman's symbol — was stamped into the upper left corner, and I cringed at the thought of the work that was inside.

"If I go back with this, I'm history," she said, tossing it onto the living-room coffee table. "Now, where was I? Oh, yeah…. Your private courier at your service, ma'am."

"Please, *please,* if you want me to fuck you," I whispered, "don't ever call me 'ma'am.' "

I had been experiencing, as I said, a lot of pent-up sexual tension, and we ripped at each other's clothes like wild beasts tearing apart their prey on some *National Geographic* special. In our ardor Jude pushed me roughly down onto the living-room floor, pulled my one-piece bathing suit down to my feet, and tied it loosely around my ankles. Next she yanked off her T-shirt and then her bikini top and fastened it around my wrists. I never realized that swimwear could double as a means of bondage, and by the time she'd finished constraining me, I was so wet with anticipation that my cunt started to ache with rhythmic throbs. That was a phrase that Lexy used a lot — "You make my cunt ache" — and I always thought she was being dramatic or young or both. Now, however, I finally got the picture.

Then Jude pushed my knees apart and dove.

The first lick was exquisitely delivered torture. She held back, watched me squirm in my restraints, then rewarded me with another. I threw my head back and squeezed my eyes closed, trying to live only in the pleasure.

"Oh…my…God," I panted. "Don't stop."

"That's my girl," she purred. "Beg me for it." Her tongue swirled my cunt like it was an ice cream cone. Where did this neophyte lesbian learn to eat pussy, and could I take lessons there too?

My knees caught her head in a vise grip, and she moaned "Oh, baby" through delicious sucking noises. I grabbed fistfuls of her hair and forced her mouth harder against my cunt until I thought I was going to implode. By this time I was gasping "Yes…yes…yes…yes," the only word my voice could manage to form as my insides turned to fire. Slowly, slowly I opened my eyes, fully expecting to see heaven.

Instead what I saw made me scream and jerk my bare ass off the floor about a foot, barely escaping the imprint of Jude's teeth in my groin.

"What are you *doing* here?" I yelled, and Jude sat up, wiping cunt juice off her chin.

"I like to watch," Lexy said smoothly, lighting up a cigarette. "Please don't stop on my account."

I never knew there were so many expletives in my vocabulary, but if I had stopped to count, there would have been a few dozen. (For the sake of good taste, they have all been deleted.) After I snapped at her to untie me, Jude sobbed through my tirade, still not sure what was happening and possibly thinking Lexy was some kinky lesbian terrorist who was going to pull an Uzi out of nowhere and obliterate us at any minute.

"Can you, like, shut her up?" Lexy asked, annoyed.

"No, I can't, *like*, shut her up," I snapped. "I want *you* out of here, *now*."

"You told me you were coming out here alone," Lexy said with less "fuck you" in her voice and more whine. "I believed you. I actually fucking believed you. Then you have the fucking nerve to bring her."

I had wanted Lexy to leave before Jude caught on to who she was and why she seemed to be so interested in whom I had sex with. But the moment of Lexy's anonymity passed.

"You're *her*?" Jude said with a caustic laugh. "You're the other one?"

"I'm not 'the other one,' honey. I predated you by *weeks*," Lexy said defiantly. Then she turned back to me. "If you didn't want to see me anymore, why couldn't you just tell me, huh? Why couldn't you be sensitive? I mean, we've had great sex, haven't we? I would've tied you up if I knew that's what you liked, and it would have been a lot better scene than this."

I couldn't believe I was in the middle of such lunacy. I decided to pretend it wasn't happening and went into my bedroom, where I threw on my John Lennon sleep shirt to cover myself. But their voices trailed after me.

"I can't believe you *lied*."

"Lynn, what the hell is going on here? What is *she* doing out here?"

At that moment I thought of closing my door and slitting my throat with my Swiss Army knife. But Harold can't stand the sight of blood, and I couldn't trust these two little divas to clean up. So I walked back out into the living room and took the chickens by the beaks.

"First of all, you have to stop referring to each other as 'her' and 'she.' It's driving me crazy. Lexy Hammond, this is Jude Mann. Jude, Lexy."

Jude shook her head, and Lexy raised her eyebrows. They both opened their mouths to speak, but I held up an authoritarian hand.

"Second, I didn't invite either one of you. You both just showed up, coincidentally and uninvited. And you, I might add," I said, pointing an accusing finger at Lexy, "conveniently brought along your own entertainment."

"Desi's just a friend," she explained with an embarrassed flush. "I...I wanted to make you jealous, and she said she could, you know, help me out."

It was my turn to shake my head. Jude's was still bobbing back and forth uncontrollably, kind of like Katharine Hepburn's, and I wondered if the whole incident had made her develop a nervous twitch that she'd have for the rest of her life. I wanted to say to Lexy, "That's sick," but the admonition from some old Sunday sermon came back to me: "Whosoever shall throw the first stone...."

Was this my punishment for harassing Claire? I wasn't raised

Catholic, so I didn't believe in any kind of sin, mortal or venial, or in divine retribution. I didn't even really believe in the divine. I hadn't been inside a church in over ten years, and that had only been to attend my sister Amy's wedding. I couldn't think of much worse, psychologically, than to find myself a lapsed Protestant with a sudden and inexplicably acute sense of Catholic guilt.

"I think we should end this little party now," I said. "I've had it."

They both looked at me with hangdog expressions. Jude's head stopped shaking, and Lexy opened her mouth to speak but closed it quickly.

"I'm going in there now to rest," I said, pointing to my bedroom. "Alone. And when I come out, please, *please* be gone. Both of you."

The bedroom door clicked behind me, and I stood with my ear pressed against the hollow wood. Their voices were faint, but I could make out part of the exchange.

"Don't let me hold you up. I can show myself out."

"I've got to make sure I have all my things."

"Well, I've gotta make a phone call."

"Go ahead. I'm not the least bit interested in listening."

I fondled the Swiss Army knife on the dresser and had an itch to turn it on them instead of myself. I pondered what motivates previously sane people to commit bloody murder. Then I put the blade down, fell onto the bed, and, amazingly, slept.

I woke to Harold and Carl talking loudly outside the bedroom door. It was dusk, and I had been sleeping for about five hours.

Groggy and disoriented from repeated and horrific dreams of Lexy aiming a gun at me and Jude standing by watching, I staggered to the door and opened it. My T-shirt was twisted, and my hair fell across my eyes.

"Lynnie! You devil!" Harold glanced past me into the bedroom. His lecherous smile faded when he saw I was alone. "Oh, we thought you were still with Jude."

"No, the little darling left quite a while ago," I said, pushing my hair aside and feeling it fall immediately back over my eyes. "Could you fix me whatever it is you're drinking?"

Carl slapped an extra gin and tonic together and handed it to me. "Don't take this the wrong way, but you look *bad*," he commented. "You okay?"

"I'm swell." I stumbled over to the sofa with the drink and collapsed like a rag doll, ready for ten or twenty more hours of sleep.

"What's with you? You two have a lovers' quarrel?" Harold asked, sitting across from me on a chair and rattling the ice in his glass. "Come on, tell Uncle Harold everything."

Carl came and plopped down next to Harold on the floor with one arm resting affectionately on his knee. Even in my misery I could see they made a cute couple. I told them just about everything, leaving out the bondage part, but Harold finally wheedled it out of me.

"My, my," he said with a knowing grin at Carl. "Straitlaced Lynn Woods discovers BDSM."

"Oh, shut up," I said. "Don't you dare use this against me."

"Wait — you're dating two women at the same time?" Carl asked, trying to catch up. "I thought lesbians never did that."

"Welcome to the '90s, my sweet," Harold said, beaming. "Not just *two* women, mind you, but two women well under the age of thirty."

"Go, girl!" Carl said.

"And Lynn will be forty-one on July 15."

"I'm warning you, Harold, shut up."

"Let me shake your hand," Carl said, reaching over to me. But I frowned at both of them and tried to ignore their relentless teasing, which had begun to feel like that old playground game, the Farmer in the Dell. At the end the last child who hasn't been picked becomes the cheese — "The cheese stands alone, the cheese stands alone. Heigh-ho-the-derry-o, the cheese stands alone!" — and all the other children form a tight circle and start thrashing her, singing gleefully, "We all pound the cheese!" I remember it vividly because I had gone through an unpopular phase during third grade, where I very often found myself as the cheese, standing alone.

Bad memories live on.

"I guess this proves that lesbians aren't very good at buddy fucking," Harold said with a sigh. "I had high hopes for you, Lynnie, but I'm afraid you just wouldn't cut it as a gay man." He and Carl burst into raucous laughter, their drinks spraying out of their mouths.

I took aim and threw a pillow at both of them, then trudged back into my room. There were still four days left to my vacation, and I decided to use them well.

So I slept.

And slept.

And slept.

The only reason I decided to get up on Wednesday at about 6 o'clock in the evening was because Harold was banging on my door.

I tried to disregard it at first, but he didn't give up. The banging was accompanied by short, curt barks of my name — "Lynn! Lynn! Lynn!" — that started to sound like machine-gun fire.

"What?" I said, opening the door. He looked half worried, half cross — like if I'd killed myself in there, should he be upset or mad?

"April Ronsard has now called five times in the last two hours," he reported. "Haven't you heard the phone ringing off the hook? I swear, I'm ready to unplug it."

"Go ahead," I said, attempting to close the door, but Harold put a foot firmly in the way to stop me.

"You've got to call her back," he insisted. "She says it's an emergency."

"Emergency, schmergency," I said. "That probably means her hairdresser canceled on her."

"She sounded really upset, Lynn," Harold continued. "I can't be sure, but she sounded like she'd been crying."

Crying? The Queen of Cool? Wouldn't it streak her oh-so-carefully-applied makeup? I felt distrustful, like it was probably just a ploy to get me back to Manhattan so she could besiege me with all her "thoughts" about lesbians and how they fit into her brand of '90s feminism.

"All right, all right," I conceded reluctantly. "Is she at home?"

Harold shrugged and handed me the number. He stood checking out me and my depression.

"You've spent two days in your room," he observed. "We all missed you on the beach."

"Too much sun's bad for you anyway," I said. "Look, this is *my* vacation. I can do whatever the fuck I want with it!"

Harold's head sagged a little, the way it always did when I snapped at him unnecessarily. He looked as if he wasn't sure what to do, strike back or withdraw until I'd come to my senses. "I'm spending the night at the Haven," he announced. "If you need me or anything."

"Great. Fine." I could be a bitch. But it wasn't really Harold I was mad at. I wasn't sure who I was mad at, but it felt like my insides were about to boil over.

"Have fun!" I called after him, softening my tone, and he smiled and waved as the screen door clacked behind him.

"This better be good," I grumbled as I punched the numbers to April's home phone. Her answering machine switched on, and I almost hung up without leaving a message. How "emergency" could the situation be if she wasn't picking up the phone? But just as "...please leave a message, and I'll get back to you when I can" was playing, April's recorded voice was interrupted by her real one.

"Lynn? Is that you?" she asked breathlessly.

"Yes, April, it's me," I replied. "What's up?"

"Is Jude there?"

"No, she left Monday afternoon. Why?"

"She hasn't been here since last Sunday!" April said in a panicked screech. "And she's not answering the phone at her apartment. I don't know where she is! Do you think she's all right?"

"Calm down, April," I said, but my own heart picked up an extra beat. "I'm sure she's fine and there's a good explanation. Have you called her mother?"

"Oh, I can't call Jill with this," April said, shocked at the suggestion. "She has an opening Friday night at Art Nouveau."

"But she might know where Jude is," I pointed out. "And save you and me a lot of grief. And if she doesn't...well, regardless of her opening, don't you think she'd want to know if her daughter's missing?"

"But I feel so responsible," April moaned. "I mean, I was looking after Jude in a way. I took her on as a favor to her mother. She's not the best assistant I ever had, but I can't tell Jill that she's gone! Not after I've been, well, a bit harsh with her lately over her work performance. Maybe I was too harsh." She took a few deep breaths. "I know this only concerns you in a very peripheral way, Lynn, but I was wondering if you could come back a few days early. This is really very serious."

Since I was more involved than April imagined, she didn't have to ask twice. In fact, while we were talking, I had already pulled out the ferry schedule and was resignedly searching for the next departure time.

I wouldn't make a very good sleuth. Even though I read mystery novels voraciously on vacation, I can almost never figure out who the killer is. I always pick the person whom the writer has deliberately set in place to foil readers. When the real killer emerges, I can't remember any of the clues that should have led me to him or her. And even after years of devouring mystery novels, I never get any better.

So though I came charging back from Cherry Grove to help locate Jude, I had no idea what I was doing. I just had a lurking suspicion that Lexy was somehow involved.

I don't want to say I suspected her of foul play. I didn't think she was an evil or psychotic person, just a tad obsessed. That's not as egotistical as it sounds. Besides her frequent phone calls and habit of appearing on my doorstep, I'd amassed a folder full of love notes from Lexy, funny, sexy postcards with pictures of naked women on them that arrived in the mail several times a week, usually signed "Guess who?" or "Your phantom lover." She'd draw conversation bubbles coming out of their mouths like in comic strips and fill them in with "You are so-o-o sexy" or "I can't wait to get my hands on you." On one photo card a vampy Mae West said, "Who do you have to fuck to get a drink around here?" — the classic line from *The Boys in the Band* that made me realize Lexy was more up on film history than I thought. All the attention was charming and endearing and immensely flattering, but it also sometimes made me worry.

Like now.

So early Thursday morning the first thing I did was call Lexy. At work I got her voice mail, and I left a pleasant, cryptic message: "Hi, I came back a few days early. Just wanted to see what's going on with you. Can we have a truce?"

Then I tried her at home, and I sat through her long message, what seemed like two whole minutes of a rap song, followed by Lexy's cool-and-groovy voice-over commanding, "Hey, come on — leave a message."

Every time I heard this message (and she hadn't changed it since I'd known her), I realized I was getting older. I could no more identify the rap singer on the message than I could translate from ancient Greek. The only rap artists I'd ever known the name of was Salt-N-Pepa — and that only because of a painful incident with my young niece. For her thirteenth birthday two years earlier, my brother Will's daughter, Marya, came to spend a weekend with me and Claire in the city. We tried to show her a good time, but I guess we were pretty out of touch with the tastes of adolescents. We took her to the Statue of Liberty, and she acted like we were forcing her to go to school on the weekend. Later we went to dinner at an Italian restaurant — don't most kids love Italian food? — and she picked her way around a cheesy order of lasagna while never saying a word. "She's a teenager now," Claire said, shrugging it off, but I missed the vibrant, full-of-life child-niece whom I had known and enjoyed.

Finally we hit pay dirt the next day when we took her shopping at Tower Records. (It's still called that, even though there isn't a record album — or barely a tape — in sight.) Marya was totally in her element, scooping up CDs like the store was going out of business. I think she even spoke, but only to say, "Wow, this is awesome!" If I had kept my mouth shut, she would have gotten her booty and we would have been home free. But *no*. I had to ask her what groups she liked and then, helpfully, inquire of a salesclerk in what was, I guess, an embarrassingly loud voice, "Excuse me, do you have anything by a group called Salt and Pepper?" Marya raised her eyebrows, threw down all the CDs she'd already selected, and rushed out onto the street, just to get the hell away from me. Little did I know until Claire informed me later that not only had I pronounced the name wrong but asking if they had "anything" by such popular performers was a little like saying, "Excuse me, do you have anything by somebody named Michael Jackson?"

I waited for the beep on Lexy's answering machine and then left the same sort of friendly message that I had at her job. Then I was at a loss for what to do next, so I sat down, smoked a few cigarettes, and thought.

And thought.

Thinking is good. At my age I find I sometimes have to ponder things quite a while before what I already know comes back to me. So in the middle of my third cigarette, I remembered the keys to Jude's apartment that she had given me once — with a "No strings, honest" disclaimer — so that I could get into her apartment if she were late arriving from April's for our date. I had forgotten to give them back to her, and they were lying on my dresser right where I'd dropped them. Did I really have the chutzpah to just burst into

Jude's apartment playing detective?

While I was weighing the pros and cons of illegal entry, April phoned to inform me she had tried to call Jude all Wednesday evening and most of Thursday morning, but there was still no answer at her apartment. April sounded a lot more mellow than the day before, but since the situation was even more serious, I wondered if she'd had her Prozac prescription refilled.

Of course, I couldn't tell April about Jude's keys, because then she would know about our affair. I muttered something to her about calling the police, then, armed with the keys and guts of steel, I took the subway to the West Sixties.

Jude's apartment building is unusual for a deluxe residence because it doesn't have a doorman, just a uniformed elevator operator. This worked in my favor, because I didn't have to be announced; I simply had to say what floor I wanted. I dressed like I was going to a meeting with April so I'd arouse less suspicion, and the elevator man never even blinked when I authoritatively instructed, "Fourth floor, please."

Just to be doubly safe, I rang the bell before I tried the key in the lock. No answer. Waiting a minute or two, then looking stealthily over both shoulders, I slipped the first key into the deadbolt and released it easily. I sighed. The second key was likewise a snap. No tricks here luckily; no keys that I had to wiggle in the lock or spit on first or lift up, then down, then up again before the lock finally yielded. (Don't laugh — Claire had a situation like that in her first New York apartment.) I took a deep breath and twisted the knob.

I was in.

Have I mentioned that I'm a big fat coward? When I told you that Harold hates the sight of blood, did I also admit that I almost

138

pass out each and every time I cut myself? I was so terrified at what I might find in Jude's apartment, my heart was beating like I had just run the New York marathon. But standing in the ballroomlike living room, I couldn't smell death, and that was a good sign. I wasn't exactly sure what death would smell like, but I knew it wouldn't be good.

"Jude?" I called out, though what good I thought that would do if she was comatose somewhere, I don't know. Still, I said it again. "Jude?"

I checked out the first floor, and there were a few signs of life. A Melitta filter filled with coffee grounds that were still wet. Toast sweat on a plate. Jude had been here that morning, for sure.

I should have left it at that, but now I was beginning to fancy myself as Jane Marple or Nancy Drew. I quietly ascended the flight of stairs to the second floor and slinked down the hallway to Jude's bedroom.

It didn't look as if she'd slept there Wednesday night. I knew from the nights I'd stayed with her that she rarely if ever made her bed, and the sheets were new and pristinely in place. Jill footed the bill for a maid who came in weekly to clean and change the linen, and it seemed as if she had been there very recently. The shades were drawn, and the room looked abandoned and forlorn.

Then I remembered what Jude had told me on our first sleepover. She slept in her room, but she fucked in Jill's. It gave her some sort of perverse thrill, even though her mother lived in a totally different place now.

Did I dare check Jill's room? I knew where it was, because Jude and I had enjoyed each other in the queen-size bed there on several occasions. Was this now overstepping the bounds of concern for Jude's well-being?

The door to Jill's bedroom was ajar, and I slipped my head in through the crack. Sure enough, the bed was a mess of sheets and pillows. Someone probably had herself a good time there the night before. I slid all the way into the room and stood at the foot of the bed, staring at the evidence of desire. You won't believe this, but I couldn't stop myself — I was actually overwhelmed with jealousy.

What suddenly popped into my mind at that moment of irrational covetousness was an aphorism I'd read several years before. Jenny Holzer is a favorite artist of mine, and she specializes in aphorisms — she engraves them on benches, she makes electronic displays out of them — and this was one of her gems. It stuck with me because it said worlds about the conundrum of desire and jealousy and obsession: "Protect me from what I want."

Unfortunately, I didn't have much time to dwell on Holzer's wisdom. The next thing I knew, there was a shriek behind me, and when I turned in surprise toward the scream, I was face-to-face with the celebrated Jill Womann. Stark naked.

When she sensed that I was simply an unarmed intruder and not a murderer, Jill stopped screaming and feigned toughness. She grabbed a robe and held it in front of her.

"I've got the phone right here," she said, picking up the cordless. I could hear her voice shake a little. "I'm calling the cops."

"Please, wait, I can explain," I begged. "I'm a friend of Jude's. Jude Mann, your daughter?" Duh! How many Judes could she possibly know? "Lynn Woods," I introduced myself, offering my hand as if we were at an art opening. "Jude and I both work for April Ronsard."

She put down the phone. "What the hell are you doing in my bedroom?" she demanded with ferocity that was now real and not put-on. "And how did you get in?"

"I...I had the keys," I stumbled, trying to be evasive but not succeeding. Knowing how she felt about Jill, I didn't think Jude would want to divulge much about her love life to her mother. "Jude gave me the keys once when we were meeting here. She thought she might be late, you see, and I just held on to them after that, but I've been meaning to give them back. Really. We really haven't known each other very long at all."

Jill Womann wasn't born yesterday, and she raised an eyebrow when she grasped what my relationship to her daughter must be. "So," she said with slight amusement, "Jude's finally discovered the pleasures of women. I wondered how long it would take. Like mother, like daughter, you know." She crossed to the bed, throwing on her silky robe and giving me a last peek at her Grecian body. It wasn't slim and girlish like Jude's but instead full, rounded in all the right places, and voluptuous. I blushed.

"What, you've never seen your lover's mother naked before?" she asked with a playful grin. She rifled through the nightstand, then approached me and extended her hand. "I'm Jill Womann. Do you have a cigarette by any chance?"

"I know who you are," I replied, taking an almost full pack out of my bag and offering it to her. She took the whole thing. "I mean, I've seen your picture in feminist art books."

"Right beside *Pudenda 12* and *Pudenda 17,* no doubt," she smiled, mocking her own early work. "My titles were *so* original, don't you think?"

"I'm no art critic," I shrugged, "but I'd say the titles don't matter. Those sculptures were very important to the feminist art movement."

"Yeah, yeah," she said, seemingly bored. She sat on the edge of the bed and took long, luxurious, appreciative puffs off the cigarette, as if she'd just deplaned from a five-hour cross-country no-smoking-allowed flight. Now I understood Jude's aversion to smoking: Her mother was hooked. "Anyway, Lynn — it's Lynn, right? — just because you've got keys doesn't explain why you decided to use them when Jude's not even here."

"Do you know where she is?" I asked excitedly.

"Of course," she said, then backed down. "Well, sort of. She's staying with a friend while I'm in town. My daughter and I...well, you probably know this already." She peered at me curiously through the cigarette smoke. "Jude and I don't always get along. When I come to town for an opening, she stays somewhere else. So to answer your question, I know she's somewhere, but I'm not sure where. There's a phone number around, but she doesn't want me to use it unless I'm dying, so I'm not even sure where I put it." Her robe gaped open in front, revealing the top of one gorgeous globe. "But you still haven't answered my question. What are you *doing* here?"

She was losing patience, so I decided I should level with her. "Well, as I mentioned, Jude and I work together—"

"Hmm," she interrupted. "Take my advice, romance and work don't mix."

"Yes, thanks. Anyway, Jude hasn't been to work since last weekend, and April is very concerned. We both are. There's been no one answering the phone here, and—"

"Oh, I can't stand phones," she explained, tugging her robe over her breast. "I turn off the ringer every chance I get. I just let the machine pick up, and then eventually I listen to the messages. Sometimes I erase them and don't even bother."

"Doesn't that make it hard for your gallery to reach you?" I wondered. "I mean, it must be very frustrating when they want to talk to you."

"Oh, after twenty years they know to do everything in person or by mail. They have messenger service and FedEx bills up the wazoo." She finished one cigarette and started another just seconds later. Jude had grown up not just with a smoker but a chain-smoker.

"Do you have any idea why Jude hasn't gone to work? Is she sick? She hasn't even called April to let her know what's going on." I desperately wanted a cigarette, but Jill had tucked my pack into the pocket of her robe.

"It's probably some rebellion against me," Jill said with disgust. "Believe me, if you get to know Jude better, you'll see how many things are a rebellion against me. I wasn't a good mother, I was away too much, I didn't focus on being Mommy, I never baked cookies, I left her father. Yadda, yadda. No matter how good she had it, no matter how many bills I pay — college, travel, a *maid*, for God's sake — it doesn't matter. Jude has a big fat antifeminist chip on her shoulders, if you ask me. I raised a goddamn *conservative*." She almost spat the word out. "I thought getting her a job with April might help. You know, April's very glamorous, and I thought Jude would like that feminists can be glamorous too. But apparently the job's not working out for her. Maybe she'd rather wait tables than be an assistant to a famous author. I don't know. I just don't know. Go figure." She ended her tirade with a wide, sweeping flourish of the hand holding the cigarette.

"Well" was all I could think to say. "Anyway."

"Yes, anyway."

I started to back toward the door, and Jill didn't notice. She was too absorbed in her own disappointment at her relationship with her daughter. "Anyway, I should be going," I said softly. "I'm sorry

I scared you. I was just very concerned about Jude. I'm glad she's okay, even though you're not sure where she is."

Jill was on her third cigarette. "That phone number might turn up somewhere," she said. "Why don't you give me your number so I can call you if I find it? You know, even if I'd mislaid it, I'm sure Jude will come to the gallery tomorrow night. You should definitely come."

"Yeah, April told me about the opening. Congratulations." I fumbled in my bag for my business card, which had my name and number and my occupation listed as "Writer." "You can reach me here or leave a message."

" 'L.J. Woods, Writer,' " Jill read from the card, holding it away from her about a foot. "Really. You said you work for April. What do you write?"

"Her books, mostly," I said, wondering if I should divulge that. Did April tell everyone she wrote her own stuff? "An occasional article or speech."

"Huh," she commented. "You're her ghostwriter. That's funny."

It may be an unusual occupation, but I would never describe it as "funny." Defensively I arched my back. "What's so funny about it?"

"Oh, nothing, really. Nothing at all. But I don't meet many ghostwriters, and I've been dating a woman who just broke up with one."

I gulped. Did I really want to know this? "Oh, yeah?" I said hesitantly. "What's her name?"

"I don't know. I make it a strict policy never to know too much about my lovers' ex-lovers." She seemed like a woman after my own heart.

"No, I mean, who are you dating? What's her name?" I persisted.

Now I *had* to know.

"A lovely woman," Jill said, a peachy glow flushing her face and neck as she thought of her new lover, who was probably the one who had helped to leave the sheets in such a twist. "Her name's Claire Ulrich. Do you know her?"

Jill claimed I fainted, but I'm not a fainter. I just got a little light-headed and had to sit down on the bed, where I lost consciousness for probably a minute, tops.

When I came to, my head was between my legs and Jill was hovering over me with a cold washcloth. "My God, Lynn, are you okay?" she asked several times as she pressed the cloth to the back of my neck.

"What happened?"

"You fainted," she said, moving the cloth to my forehead as I sat up. "You looked like a balloon deflating. Thank God, you made it to the bed!"

"You're dating Claire Ulrich?" I asked, suddenly remembering what had brought on my attack. "You're dating Claire Ulrich?" My tone rose to an accusatory pitch, and Jill withdrew the cool cloth.

"That's what I said," she replied curtly. "She's art-directing the catalog for the new show."

"Well, I'm her ghostwriter," I said. "I mean, I'm the one. Claire and I...I'm the one." I wasn't making much sense, but I figured she'd get the picture. I was certainly starting to.

I understood now why Claire had made such a sudden transformation in her appearance. She was dating a famous artist, whose elegant silk bathrobe was printed with a delirious swirl of purples and golds. Jill was probably at the root of Claire's newfound desire to be perfectly color-coordinated and look the role of art director.

"Well," Jill said, staring at me sideways. "Isn't this a coincidence? You're sleeping with the daughter of your ex-lover's new lover." With that she lit another cigarette and offered me one, which I took gratefully. "Don't you just love lesbians?"

"Actually, this is the one thing about lesbians that I despise," I snarled. "I hate it how many people actually get into bed with you." It was a ridiculous statement, I knew. Straight women carry around just as much sexual and emotional baggage as lesbians, and straight and gay men have it too. They just seem to care less.

"Hmm," she said, smiling in a wistful way. "This makes me nostalgic for the '70s, when we were all fucking each other but nobody would dream of calling it 'fucking.' "

My throat felt like sandpaper, so I extinguished my cigarette and dug a roll of Life Savers out of my bag. "Tropical fruits," I said. "Want one?"

Jill wrinkled up her nose as if I'd just offered her a nice helping of dog shit. She contentedly puffed away.

"Listen, I don't know what Claire has told you, but it's not true," I said, rushing to preserve what little face I had. After all, I met Jill when I illegally entered her apartment. How could she not think that every bad thing Claire ever said about me was absolutely true?

"Oh, she really hasn't told me anything," Jill replied casually. But she turned her face away so I couldn't read it. "I told you, I don't like all that ex-lover hoo-ha. I really have much better things to do."

"I'm sure you do," I said, noting the defensiveness in her tone. I stood up, still feeling a little shaky but desperate to be out of that bedroom. I was sitting on the *sheets,* for God's sake. "Look, now I really have to go."

"Yeah, okay, let me see you out."

"No need," I said. "I've been here before, remember? Oh, here are the keys." I tossed them onto the bed, and Jill made no move to fish them from the folds of the sheets. I figured the maid would find them. "Let me know if Jude's number turns up."

"Hmm," she said, obviously deep in thought about something else. I had no way of knowing what, and frankly, I didn't want to. I'd had enough "sharing" for the day.

Maybe for the entire month of July.

I called April with the news that Jude was alive but ill. I decided to try a stalling technique in case Jude had in fact lost her mind and really didn't intend to sabotage her job. April would fire her in a minute if she realized Jude was just blowing her off.

But my plan didn't work. "Oh, the nerve," April said, immediately on the offensive. I realized too late that the only thing that could have saved Jude from immediate dismissal was if she had actually been dead. "She could have had *someone* call. Anyone. All this fuss and worry for nothing! I should have fired her two weeks ago, when I first had problems with her. I didn't have to hire her, you know. I had another candidate, but Jill called and asked for a personal favor. I have no choice but to let Jill know it didn't work out, hard as I tried. I blame Jill in a way. She has always overindulged that girl, and Jude just doesn't understand the meaning of responsibility. Well, I'm going to leave a message for Jude right now, firing her."

"Don't you want to wait and talk to her?" I suggested. "Maybe there's a good explanation why Jude didn't—"

Since I was the one who had talked April out of firing Jude earlier, I didn't have much of a leg to stand on. "I can't wait! I need an assistant, and I need one now!" By April's frantic tone of voice, I could tell she must be having her usual difficulty with office machines. Though April's home office was enviably equipped with a state-of-the-art fax, photocopier, paper shredder, multimedia computer with high-speed modem and CD-ROM drive, laser printer, and flatbed scanner, she had never bothered to learn how to use any of them. She even had difficulty negotiating call waiting on her phone and was prone to ignoring the beeping signal when another call was coming through. "They can call back," she'd say, annoyed and missing the point of the service altogether.

What else could I do? I thought I should get off the phone quickly, before April turned her wrath on me. "Well, I gotta go," I said. "I have a million things—"

"Did you look over the materials Jude brought out to you? What did you think?" she demanded.

"I haven't had a chance," I confessed. "What with Jude's disappearance and all—"

April sighed deeply, and I briefly expected her to can me too while she was on a head-chopping roll. But our first book together had brought her too much attention and success (and money), and I knew she was superstitious about changing horses midrace. However, she might start searching for a new me for the next project if she suspected that I was losing my edge.

"Well, since the Jude incident is over, I expect you'll get right to it?" she asked rhetorically. "Why don't you come with me to Jill's opening tomorrow, and we can discuss it. It's just one of the biggest events at Art Nouveau in ages! Jill hasn't had a show in five years. Gloria will be there and Bella and Betty. Everyone's *dying* to find out if Jill has completely sold out and abandoned feminist art."

The thought of seeing Claire with Jill made my stomach churn.

And there was no way to explain how I'd met Jill Womann and gotten my own half-baked invitation. "I don't think—"

"Oh, come on, Lynn, you can be my 'date.' Won't that make people's tongues wag? They'll think I'm switching sides!"

I graciously ignored her implication that lesbianism was a "side" you could pick, like the Knicks or the Yankees. I knew there had to be a reason she was pressing me so hard, since April had never wanted to "date" me before. "What about Arthur?" I asked pointedly. Arthur was her "companion," a retired stockbroker whose main occupations seemed to be escorting April to gala events and fishing for marlin off the Florida Keys in his private yacht.

"Arthur's in Washington, the poop — his youngest daughter just had a baby or something — and I hate to go to these things alone! Oh, please! It'll be fabulous."

"But I really—"

"You don't have other plans, do you?"

The fact was, after weeks of nonstop dating, I suddenly found myself with nothing to do and no one to do it with. Even Harold, my old reliable standby, was still at the beach with his new honey.

"No," I admitted, wishing I could lie but fresh out of excuses. "Not a thing. Why don't I meet you there?"

Since I'd left the island, I'd been too busy to be despondent, but now the weight of despair bore down on me again. I tried to work. I pulled out the "material" April had sent via Jude and found it to be offensive medical "evidence" that something in the genetic makeup of lesbians indicated an "abnormality" that made them behave like straight men instead of women. If April intended to cite this in *Pink and Blue*, I regretted that I'd ever approached her about including material on lesbians. The more thoughts she had on the subject, the more likely it was that I wasn't going to be able to stand working for her.

Defeated, I put everything away, grabbed some money, and went to Ben's, a local café where you can sit for hours with a cup of coffee and a toasted bagel and no one will bother you. It was one of my favorite places to think. It has none of the pretension of the trendy coffee bars that have sprung up in my neighborhood and everywhere, the ones with exposed brick and uncomfortable chrome stools, where everyone's trying so hard to be creative that they actually exude an air of frustration.

When I say "no one will bother you" at Ben's, I mean the management won't ask you to leave or buy something else because you're occupying a table too long. You may, however, be bothered by any number of outpatients from Bellevue Hospital, which is just a few blocks away. They wander over from their drug treatments and sit mumbling to themselves and staring at other customers. These harmless crazy people have never really fazed me, and the clerks don't seem to mind them either, but I've seen some patrons become visibly upset, particularly women carrying Gucci tote bags with pedigree dogs in tow.

I ordered my usual — an everything bagel, lightly buttered, with a cup of coconut coffee — and took my favorite seat by the window, where I could watch the activity on the street. There's always something to look at. Lots of cute babies and dogs. A swarm of preschoolers with their day-care teachers desperately trying to keep track of them. Homeless people collecting cans and bottles for the deposit money. A gay couple who had probably slept together for the first time saying good-bye shyly at the corner.

But that day I saw something I had never witnessed in New York before. A gray-haired woman in a striped hospital gown and paper slippers was wheeling her own IV unit across Second Avenue, making her way boldly away from Bellevue. Her chin was raised, her lips curved into a small grin, and she was mumbling something to herself — encouragement, maybe? Some pedestrians turned to stare at her, and one car honked, but no one tried to stop her. She kept walking determinedly west, and though I stood up to get a better view, I finally lost sight of her.

I can't really explain what happened next. Maybe it was because the full impact of Claire's leaving me finally got a chance to hit me *pow!* in the gut. Maybe it was that my forty-first birthday was a just little over a week away and I had come to a point in my life when I couldn't write other people's stories anymore. Whatever it was, at that moment I so completely identified with the hospital escapee that my head was flooded with words.

I jumped up and asked one of the clerks if I could borrow a pen. He knew me as a regular at Ben's and kindly offered me his black Bic, which had prominent tooth marks in the plastic cap and a clot of ink at the tip. He didn't have any paper to lend, though, and I had to resourcefully make do with the stack of paper napkins sitting in the middle of my table. Scribbling furiously onto napkins, I must have looked like a Bellevue outpatient myself, because the young mother and toddler occupying the table next to mine suddenly got up and moved clear across the room.

I didn't care. A word had alighted in my head like the angel descending on Prior Walter in the last moments of *Angels in America: Millennium Approaches.* It was a word that had only recently taken on multiple meanings in my life — desire, aging, and fear all at the same time. The obedient scribe, I jotted it down, blots of gooey ink filling in the vowels. I read the title back to myself in awe: *"Chicken.* A Play in Three Acts by L.J. Woods."

I lost track of how many hours I stayed at Ben's, drinking coffee and writing, writing and drinking coffee. I ran out of napkins pretty quickly, and the nice clerk who lent me the pen found a pad of yellowing, unused employment forms in the office that I could write on the back of. "You can thank me in the acknowledgments," he smiled. "My name's Steven Rich. That's Steven with a *v*, Rich as in if-I-were-I-wouldn't-be-working-here. I'm an actor in real life." I pictured him sharing the story with friends — how he, a struggling young actor, helped me, a struggling middle-aged writer, to complete my first full-length play.

When I finally wandered back to my apartment, my whole body was buoyant, and I floated up the stairs instead of trudging the way I usually did, winded after just two flights. My answering machine was in the middle of picking up a message, and I expected it to be April, loading some new demands onto my back. If it was, I would courageously lift the receiver and tell her to fuck herself — that's how good I felt. I turned up the sound and listened.

"…and the number for Jude is 555-0908. If you speak to my dear daughter, would you tell her…."

I flipped the sound off and drooped onto the sofa. I recognized Jill Womann's voice, the Brooklyn accent varnished over by years in the sophisticated Manhattan art world.

But that wasn't what made me suddenly feel more like a sandbag than a balloon. It was that I had instantly recognized the phone number where Jude was staying. I'd called Lexy too many times not to know it by heart.

Not once had I made the trek down to Little Italy to visit Lexy's apartment. We always stayed at my place because Lexy had a room-mate named Svati, who had broken up with her lover of six years and spent a lot of time in the apartment trying to recover. Thursday night, when I appeared at the door, Svati was at home.

"Lexy's not here," she said, leaving the security chain on the door and talking to me through the two-inch crack. "How did you get in downstairs? Was the front door open again?"

"Wide open," I replied. "You should report it to someone. It isn't safe."

Svati sighed deeply, like someone who had tried one too many times to get the landlord to take a greater interest in building security.

"Is Jude here?" I asked.

"She's not here either."

"Is she living here now or something?"

Svati frowned at me and placed a suspicious hand on her hip. "Who *are* you, anyway? And what is it with all these questions? I don't have to answer them, you know."

"I'm sorry, Svati—"

"And how the hell do you know my name?" She stared at me fiercely with intense black eyes.

"Look, I'm Lynn Woods, Lexy's—"

"You're Lynn?" The door closed in my face. I was just about to knock again, indignantly, when I heard the chain being slid out of its track, and the door opened wide. "I can't believe I finally get to meet the mystery woman. Lexy talks about you all the time. Some of us have been teasing her that she just made you up."

"Well, here I am, in the flesh."

Svati motioned me into the apartment. I stood in the narrow, cramped hallway with her while she replaced the chain, a deadbolt, and an elaborate door-blocking device that I recognized from subway ads as the Door Club. "There's been a lot of gang violence in this neighborhood lately. People are scared," she explained as she fastened the club into place, but she didn't have to. I understood completely, being a bit obsessed with apartment security myself.

"How much did that cost?" I asked. "Do you like it?"

"Oh, it's the best investment I've made in this rattrap. It was only $49.95. I recommend it."

The place was actually larger than mine but in much worse condition. In the living room were water stains that made the walls look like they had acute psoriasis, and there was a window cracked in two places and simply taped together. The decor was indeed "early vegetable crate," as Lexy had told me on our first date. Several small crates were covered with homemade cushions and served as chairs, and one long broccoli crate was turned on its side as a coffee table. There was a rolled-up futon against one wall that seemed to be somebody's bed.

I sat on a crate. It felt a bit like when I'd sat shivah with the families of friends who'd died.

"I'd offer you tea, but we're in a rent strike, and they turned off the cooking gas," Svati said.

"How do you eat?"

"Out," she said simply, taking the crate across from mine. "How about a Coke?"

"No, thanks." I glanced around at the stained walls, which had the remnants of purple streamers taped to them.

"Gay Pride party. Sorry you missed it. It was amazing." Lexy hadn't told me anything about a party. She had tried to get me to meet her friends too many times and had apparently given up trying.

"Didn't you have some family thing that day?"

"Yeah, I had a family thing," I agreed, not wanting to get into the Chappaqua incident when there were more important things to talk about, like where the fuck Lexy and Jude were and why Jude was staying here.

"Oh, I remember now. A friend of yours was coming out to his family and asked you to go with him!" Svati said.

I really didn't want to take grief from Svati about this when I'd already taken it from Lexy. "Right. Now where—"

"So how'd it go?" she asked with genuine interest. "You both made it through, I guess. How did he break the news to them?"

She seemed so intrigued by Harold's story and such a willing audience that I found myself relating the day in detail while she laughed and said "Wow!" in all the appropriate places. Lexy hadn't wanted to know anything about that day because she had been so mad at me for going away. I accepted Svati's offer of a Coke finally just to have a reason to stay longer.

"What a great story!" Svati enthused. "You should write it down. You're a writer, aren't you?"

"Well, not that kind of writer, but...." An image of myself scrawling on napkins popped into my head. "...I hope to be. I'm writing a play." I blushed. I could have gone on and on but wasn't sure how much Svati really wanted to hear. I realized suddenly that I had been flirting with her a little, and she with me. She had dark, deep-set eyes and a heart-shaped face that tended to tilt slightly when she listened intently. *How old is she,* I wondered — *twenty-eight?* At least, I reasoned, the women I felt attracted to were increasingly older. Maybe the next one would even top thirty.

"That story would be great in a play! I can visualize it, I really can." Svati smiled shyly and pushed an unruly wave of short dark hair out of her eyes. "I'm working on a screenplay myself, so we have something in common. It's about an Indian lesbian who lives in Little Italy and wants to be a writer. Sound familiar? Lexy wants to direct it. Of course, she wants to direct *everything*. You know how she is." She raised a skeptical eyebrow, like she'd heard more than her fair share of Lexy's movie dreams. "We're not lovers, in case you're wondering," she added quickly. "Never have been."

"No, I, well…no, I wasn't wondering that," I said, though the thought had crisscrossed my mind a couple of times. "What I *am* wondering, though, is what Jude is doing here."

Svati's earnest smile faded when she sensed I was more interested in Lexy and Jude than I was in her. "Oh, yeah, Jude," she said with a trace of annoyance. "I don't know really. She showed up here with Lexy on Tuesday night, and she's been here ever since."

"Tuesday night?" I said, confused because I'd kicked them out of the cottage on July 4, a Monday. "You're sure it wasn't Monday?"

"No, it was definitely Tuesday. I have my writing group Monday night until 10, so I'm out late, and I was home watching a movie the night they breezed in from Fire Island."

"And they were getting along?" I asked, having trouble figuring out the situation. "They were friendly with each other?"

"Friendly?" Svati laughed, a brief, amused snort. "I'd say so. I haven't seen anyone suck face like that since—" She cut herself off abruptly when my mouth dropped open, like the hinges on my jaw had just let go. "Oh, Lynn, wow, I'm sorry. I just thought…I mean, I assumed…. You and Lexy have an open relationship, don't you? I mean, after her bout with monogamy with the girlfriend from hell, Lexy swore never again."

"She did, huh?"

"Yeah, the evil Moira practically ripped her heart out. You know she was having phone sex long distance with an ex-lover, then stick-ing Lexy with the bill?" Lexy had left the phone sex part out of the story when she relayed it to me, though I probably should have guessed. Maybe it had embarrassed her to be so completely cuck-olded.

"To answer your question, yeah, we leave things open," I said, smirking. "And by the way, so do Jude and I."

It was Svati's turn to lose control of her facial muscles. "Wow, I didn't realize—"

"In fact," I continued, "both my relationships are so wide open that maybe I should just walk right out of them."

Svati watched me silently, tossing her hair back again. Have I mentioned that I'm a sucker for a woman with untamed hair? I pondered for a moment whether, if I asked Lexy's roommate out, it would be because she was so cute and seemingly willing or because it would rile Lexy and Jude. I wasn't really sure.

"I know this is sort of spontaneous," I ventured, "but how'd you like to go get a drink or something to eat? You know, *out.*"

"I'd like that a lot," she answered, jumping up. "I'm feeling kind of spontaneous myself."

I know what you're thinking. Such a nice girl, Svati, sitting at home trying to mend her broken heart. How could I take advantage of her vulnerability?

Well, I'm happy to report that I didn't put the moves on her. We went to a nearby dive and drank a couple of beers in a booth with gashed vinyl seats, and I told her the whole story of the Lynn-Lexy-Jude triangle and the Lynn-Claire-Jill-Lexy-Lynn connection. She was an avid listener. Then she related her own harrowing story of

Riki, her lover of six years who decided to go straight and was now engaged to a man.

Both of us broke all the dating rules by talking about ex-lovers, but in a way I found it liberating to unload everything right away, lay all my cards out among the beer spills on our table. We stayed at the joint until after midnight; then I walked her home and grabbed a taxi. All I got was a quick chaste peck on the lips.

"When you've untangled your love life," Svati said sweetly, "I'd really like to see you again. But I can't take any high dyke drama right now. Riki left almost five months ago, and it's taking me a while to regroup."

She was smart, I thought, to give herself plenty of breathing room. Maybe that's what I had done wrong. Claire — whom I had expected to be my life partner — had been gone only a few months, and I was already trying to negotiate a three-ring love circus. No wonder things had spun out of control. I found myself wishing that I had met Svati first instead of Lexy. She seemed so incredibly grounded in her own needs.

"You're wise beyond your years," I smiled. "How old are you anyway?" I had to ask, even though it didn't matter. Svati seemed more self-knowledgeable than I was, whatever her birth date.

"Oh, God," she said, laughing, "Lexy told me you were like this."

"Like what?" I grinned.

"Ageist. And you really are, aren't you?"

I colored with embarrassment and started to stammer that I withdrew the question, that her age made no difference whatsoever.

But to my amazement, she answered it. "I'll be thirty in October."

Yes!

159

I should have felt better. Lexy and Jude were taking care of themselves, and the prospect of dating Svati — or possibly someone like
Svati — was like a smog-free dawn rising over Manhattan. Harold
had a new love interest too after years of loneliness. I could finally
get back to a more normal life (whatever that was), write a play, take
an interest in my job, see friends, maybe even start answering my
phone again instead of lurking in the shadows, screening calls.

Then why did I feel bad? Things were falling so neatly into place.

I knew what it was, but I didn't particularly want to face it.

Starts with a *C,* ends with an *e,* and has *l-a-i-r* in the middle.

The American Heritage Dictionary defines "lair" as "the den or
dwelling of a wild animal." But its second definition, the Scottish
meaning (and we Woodses are Scottish through and through), is "a
tomb or grave."

I'm a writer; I look these things up. Maybe I shouldn't.

We had made a life together. I'll admit, it wasn't perfect, but it
was a decent life. We had our apartment, our friends, our rituals.
We even had a private commitment ceremony five years ago in
which we exchanged rings, thin gold bands from Tiffany's that we

splurged on, 300 bucks apiece. We went on a honeymoon to the Catskills and didn't leave our rustic inn for three days.

In my riotous young lesbian days, when I was hopping from bed to bed like they were squares on a checkerboard, I never thought lesbians had lasting relationships. I certainly didn't know anybody who'd been together for more than a couple of months. Then, it was the thrill of seducing someone, of getting her into bed, of finding out who else she'd slept with and swapping names like bubble-gum cards. Once I had been a link in a lesbian daisy chain that connected me all the way to Rita Mae Brown. I had slept with Hilary, who slept with Janine, who slept with Kit, who slept with Georgia, who slept with Penny, who slept with Diana, who slept with Rita Mae. You get the picture.

Then I met Claire, and it seemed possible for relationships to last longer than a tube of toothpaste. Claire and I had a mutual friend, Joanne, who thought we might be good together, so she gave me Claire's number. We arranged a blind date at Sandolino's, a Village restaurant that doesn't exist anymore but that had great sandwiches and omelets and killer soups. You could eat really well for under five bucks, which was important to both of us because we were young and just starting out in our careers. I remember Claire asking on the phone, "How will we know each other?" and me replying that we'd just know. Then I appeared holding a red rose in my teeth. She had been waiting for ten minutes, reading something by Adrienne Rich, and she glanced up from her book, saw the rose, and her face exploded into one hugely winning smile.

We moved in together two months later. That was how it started.

How it ended, you already know. But it was all the stuff in between — thirteen years of everyday stuff, both good and bad: romantic dinners at home, holidays with homophobic families, movie dates on Friday night, arguments that I haven't told you about — that made it impossible for me to feel good. I missed her. I missed things about her that had driven me crazy. The thought of starting all over again with someone else made me want to shrivel into a dust bunny and blow away. Was this all there was to life, starting over and over and over?

If Harold had been in town, he would have said, "Snap out of it!" But he wasn't, so I indulged myself in a wash of self-pity, getting more and more maudlin as Friday morning wore on. At one horrible moment I even scrutinized my face in the bathroom mirror to see how much pain I was in. It registered plainly in deep forehead grooves and puffy pink eyes.

Then the phone rang, and things just got worse. It was Lexy.

Instead of saying "Hello," the way most people do, Lexy said, "I'll bet you're wondering what's going on."

"You know, Lexy, yesterday I was," I admitted. "Today I don't think I really care."

"Frankly, my dear, you don't give a damn?"

"Something like that."

"I want to explain anyway," Lexy insisted. Her voice lowered to a barely audible whisper. I had never seen her office, but I'd visited enough big publishing companies to know the general layout: vast spaces subdivided into six-by-six cubicles with only chin-high panels as walls. Everybody could hear everything if they wanted to, and they usually wanted to.

"Svati told me you dropped by," Lexy continued. I had to strain to hear her, pushing the receiver hard against my ear. "It isn't what you think."

"What do I think it is?" I asked coolly, not giving an inch.

"You think we planned the whole thing to hurt you," Lexy said.

"And you didn't."

"Right. It just happened." There was a semi-silence in which I heard the background sounds of her office — voices talking, phones ringing, papers rustling. It reminded me of listening to the fund-raising pledge drive at National Public Radio. "You know, we left the cottage together, and, I don't know, we just started talking and talking. I guess we both realized we weren't, like, monsters, that we actually had a lot in common."

"You and Jude have a lot in common?" I said, amazed. It was hard to picture them together, the baby leather dyke and the Vassar girl.

"Well, for one thing we were both totally intimidated by *you*."

"And that's my fault?"

"No, I didn't mean that," she added quickly. "But I'm not sure either one of us could have ever gotten what we, you know, needed."

I waited for some sort of explanation or conclusion. I was too drained from my own pity party to ask her any probing questions.

"A friend of mine is studying to be a psychologist." Uh-oh, a student therapist. "And he says Jude and I both have these mother issues, and that's why we were going out with you."

She made it sound like they had melded into one person. I knew about Jude's mother issues, but Lexy had never given me a clue about hers. In fact, I didn't recall that she'd ever mentioned *having* a mother. Maybe that was because of her issues. Whatever, it was definitely too late in the game for me to hear about them now.

"And that you have a fear of getting old, some sort of midlife thing, so that's why you were going out with us."

Okay, enough of this pop psychology.

"Anyway, I can't really explain what happened, but it was just like Jude and I clicked and, well, I don't know. I don't know."

"And now you're together," I stated numbly.

"Not really, no. Well, for the moment, yes. I mean, I'm not sure we were, like, predestined to be together for life. But I do think there was a reason that we finally met." She said to someone else, "Just a minute — I'll be right there."

"Do you have to go?" I asked hopefully.

"Yeah, sort of. I mean, yeah. My boss just poked her head in. I called in sick the last couple of days; I just couldn't face coming in, and now I'm going to pay. The first thing she said to me today was 'You look well, Lexy' with this, you know, attitude."

"So you should go."

"Jude wants to talk to you too," she added. "Just to square things. She'll probably call you up or something."

"Why am I not surprised?"

"Do you have to be so goddamn cold?" she snapped suddenly. "I mean, can't you say, 'I can see where you're coming from'?"

"I can see where you're coming from," I repeated obediently.

"Oh, that's sincere."

I lit a cigarette. I think I meant it to torture her a little, since I knew working in a smoke-free office was agonizing.

"So, I guess, maybe…well…I'll see you around?" she asked.

"Yeah, sure, maybe," I said noncommittally. "But I have to warn you. I'm not one of those dykes who stays friends with all the women she's ever slept with."

"Why am I not surprised?" she mimicked.

After Lexy's call I brought a mug of coffee and my pack of Marlboro's down to the front stoop of my apartment building and sat on the steps.

Stoop sitters are fixtures in Brooklyn, but you don't see them much in Manhattan except, for some reason, on my block. I'm a big stoop sitter myself, especially when I feel lonely. I really needed someone to talk to, but I didn't know who to turn to. Beth would just convey all my woes to Claire, and my pride would never allow that. Harold was the perfect choice, but who knew what he was doing and when exactly he would come back from doing it? I was actually toying with the idea of going back inside and, in desperation, calling my mother when the front door opened and Alec, with *The New York Times* tucked under a skinny arm, shuffled out in his slippers and baggy shorts to enjoy the late-morning sun.

"Alec!" I called out. "You're out and about! How are you?"

"Well, the trip downstairs was okay, but I might need some help getting back up," he said, looking relieved that someone he knew was there to help him. "If you can, that is. I don't know what I was thinking, coming all the way down here." I supported his arm as he lowered himself onto the stoop.

"Sure," I said. "You want to rest for a while?"

"Yeah, a couple of minutes, since I came all this way," he sighed. "It just looked so nice and sunny out, I couldn't resist. Don't tell Jon, okay? He's very protective of my energy. And he doesn't think I ever use enough SPF 45." He glanced at my cigarettes like he really wanted one, then averted his eyes. "So you're back from the Grove early. Tell me everything. How was the vacation? Isn't that house funky?"

"That's a good word for it," I agreed. "Everything was…great."

He stared at me sideways, unconvinced. There had been too big a gap between "was" and "great" to convince anyone, and even tired and sick, Alec was sharp as a pin.

"What happened? You and Harold have a fight?"

"No, actually, he met a nice guy, and I expect him to come back with plans for his commitment ceremony," I said. "Can't you see it? Freda Chews in a white satin train."

"White isn't her color," Alec said, frowning. "Her complexion's too creamy. She'll have to go for ecru. So Harold hit the jackpot, huh?"

"With a little help from me, of course."

"Of course. And what about you? Did you hit anything?"

"A dead end?" I suggested, smiling. "Rock bottom? A brick wall?"

"Lynn, this was supposed to be a vacation, not an accident," Alec said, laughing and coughing at the same time. "Come to think of it, you look a little worse for wear. Do you want to talk about it?"

I did want to talk about it, I *needed* to talk about it — but Alec looked like he was ready for a nap, and I thought he would need his strength for the trek back upstairs. More to the point, I always feel like I shouldn't burden sick friends with my trivial problems, even if they offer to listen to them. Like my losing Claire and then two casual lovers in one fell swoop and experiencing a minor midlife crisis could never, ever compare to having AIDS, so therefore I should just say that everything's fine. The problem is, that becomes very lonely and superficial.

"Let me just ask you this," I said, switching gears. "You and Jon have been together, what, eighteen years or so? You were living here when I moved in, so it's definitely more than fifteen."

"Our eighteenth anniversary's in September," he smiled softly, some almost-forgotten memory darting through his mind. "That was a great time. We had both just started teaching at the same high school, and we met at a teachers in-service day. We had lunch, and lunch expanded into dinner, and then it was suddenly time for breakfast. Three square meals. We've been together ever since."

"So how have you done it? I know I've asked you this before, but how have you two managed to keep going all these years?"

166

He glanced down at the *Times* as if the answer were printed there. "I don't know, really. Luck?" he proposed with an impish shrug. "Good timing?"

"Good timing?" I repeated, confused.

"Yeah, you know, sometimes you just meet a person at the right time in your life and his life and it all comes together. That's sort of luck and timing combined, I guess."

Luck and timing. It sounded like the same formula an acquaintance of mine, a stand-up comic, had told me was the route to her success in New York's comedy clubs. "Oh, great. I have awful timing," I said, shaking my head. "And terrible luck."

"No, you don't," Alec countered. "Weren't you sitting here wishing for someone to talk to, and then I appeared?"

"You're right," I admitted. I couldn't help smiling. "Maybe this was a sign that my luck's going to change."

I almost believed it for a minute. Standing up, I offered Alec an arm to help him off the stoop. But as we fumbled together through the front door, I looked back over my shoulder and noticed that the sky was clouding up.

In the mail was a card from Claire, an announcement of Jill's art opening with a personal note appended. "Lynn — Jill told me you met. Small world, isn't it? Will I see you here? Best, Claire."

The timing was unbelievable. Jill must have called her immediately with the news, and Claire must have run to the post office with the invitation. Manhattan is known for its bad postal service. Once I mailed a birthday card to Harold three days in advance, just to make sure he got it, and it showed up in his mail three weeks later. Only bills and rent-increase notices seem to come on time — bad news travels fast? Bills, rent increases, and notes from ex-lovers.

I read the note a couple of times. I hated her breezy tone. "Best, Claire." Best what? I'm skeptical of people who use "Best" as a closing. I think they do it because they're afraid to say "Love" and need some innocuous way to end a note. Personally, when I don't know what to put at the end, I write in a string of X's and O's. They're casual, noncommittal, and everybody knows you don't really want to hug and kiss them that many times.

I turned the postcard over. "New Work by Jill Womann: *The Power Series*" appeared under a photograph of a metal sculpture that looked a little like a twisted penis. Maybe I was just reading into it, or maybe I have some weird fascination with penises that a psychoanalyst would have a field day with.

There were also some fund-raising appeals in the mail and a birthday card from my kid sister, Amy, who is chronically early for everything. She blames the example of our father, who used to make us all pile into the car for church on Sunday morning a half hour before services began, when we lived only a five-minute drive away. We were always the first ones there, and we'd sit for fifteen or twenty minutes until some other families started wandering in. My brother, Will, and I rebelled at some point and developed our own styles: I'm always exactly on time, and Will is perpetually twenty minutes late.

Amy's card, which was a week early, had Matisse's goldfish-bowl painting on the front and a sweet, handwritten message inside: "Have a wonderful day!" Amy had learned her lesson. Last year, when she sent me a card with big 40's printed all over it in varying typefaces, I gently chastised her. "It's time to start sending birthday cards with pretty vases of flowers or animals on them," I advised. "You're only thirty-two, so you don't understand."

April's publicist, Dee Dee Forman, had sent me a press release about *Skin Deep*. It was now being translated into Romanian and Urdu, making a total of thirty languages in which April's thoughts and my words could be read. Dee Dee had scrawled across the bottom of the release, "Isn't this *fabulous*?" reminding me of April. If I didn't know better, I'd have thought April and Dee Dee were the same person. Or maybe there was just some school you could go to learn how to be a "fabulous" person. Dee Dee had also added, "Can't *wait* to read *Pink and Blue*!"

I could wait. I had lost all interest in working with April, but maybe I had never had much desire for it in the first place. For a long time I had tricked myself into believing that writing books for other people on pop feminism and pop environmentalism and pop this-and-that was where my true talents lay. "Shadow artists," one writing book calls people like me, people who want to create their own work but are too afraid, so they do peripheral things. "Ghostwriter" was an apt title for me: I was just a figment of my own imagination.

I threw everything away, the note from Claire, the fund-raising mail, the notice from Dee Dee — everything except Amy's card, which I propped up on a bookshelf. But Matisse's goldfish stared out at me, lost and uncertain, so I took it down almost immediately and stuffed it into my desk drawer.

I was getting dressed for Jill's opening when someone pushed the downstairs buzzer to my apartment, startling me. The only people who ever came to my door without calling in advance were Jehovah's Witnesses and the UPS delivery person.

"It's me — Harold," Harold said through the crackling static of the intercom. "Can I come up?"

When I opened the door, he came straight into the apartment, hardly looking at me, and sat down heavily on the sofa. "Well, I ended it," he announced.

"With Carl?" I asked. I'd known him long enough to figure out his shorthand. I'd also been half expecting a sudden case of cold feet from Harold. "But why? You seemed to get along so well."

"He was rushing me," Harold said with an impatient scowl. "I can't be rushed."

"What did he do, ask you to marry him?" I laughed.

"No, nothing like that," he admitted. "But he asked me to have dinner tomorrow night. We just got *back*."

"Explain something to me, Harold," I said evenly. "In the Grove you spent every second with this guy for days on end. Now you

170

come back and think that seeing him tomorrow night is too rushed. Is that what you're saying?"

"Exactly," Harold replied, ignoring the irony of the situation. "We're back from Oz, Lynn. This is my *life*. This is Kansas."

"This is panic," I said. "This is being a big chicken. You don't have to end it just because you're scared or nervous. You could compromise, you know. Why don't you make a date for Sunday?"

He shook his head firmly. "Can't," he said, still not looking up. "My parents actually invited me for brunch. My mother sent me this letter telling me how much she still loved me, and my father wrote, 'We miss you, son' at the bottom. I've *got* to go."

"That's great, Harold! So you can see Carl when you get back that night."

"Can't." Harold didn't bother to elaborate on his second "can't."

"Harold, remember what you told me when I started dating Lexy? When I was scared out of my mind to take it any further?" I pursued.

"I probably said, 'Go girl'?"

"Yeah, well, you probably did, but you were even more profound than that. You said I didn't have to be looking for another spouse, that there was nothing wrong with just living a little. So now I'm giving you back the same advice. Carl's cute, he's fun, you like him. Live a little. See him Sunday. Or Monday or Tuesday. Just see him, for God's sake."

Harold blinked hard at me. "Didn't *we* get it all together since Wednesday? The last time I saw you, you were a candidate for shock therapy. You'd been hibernating in your room for days because your two little girl-toys were out of control. Did something happen I should know about?"

"Lots of things," I sighed. "You won't *believe*." I sat down next to him and draped an arm around his shoulder. "For starters Claire's dating Jill Womann, the mother of Jude, my girlfriend, who's now dating Lexy, my other girlfriend. Now I want to date Lexy's roommate, but she's putting me off until I clean up my messy love life. Yesterday I decided I should quit my job, and oh, yeah, I started to write a play."

Harold's eyes glazed over. "Wait, back up and take it one at a time."

"Can't," I said, realizing that I needed to get dressed. The outfit I had planned to wear had looked all wrong when I tried it on, too loose and baggy, making me appear to be ten pounds heavier and five years older. I had thirty minutes to find something better, and, as usual, my closet wasn't offering up many possibilities. I needed to look casual, chic, and fabulous all at the same time. "I'm getting ready to go to Jill Womann's art opening."

Harold bounced up off the sofa like a man in a wheelchair at a tent meeting who is suddenly cured. "Please, please, *please* take me. I can't miss this. I'll buy you dinner. Please?"

"I never knew you were such a Jill Womann fan," I commented skeptically. "When did this happen? I didn't think you knew much about art at all, let alone feminist art."

"Oh, I'm not a fan," he reassured me. "Gigantic vulvas are fine, but.... It's just that I can't miss the chance to see all the players in your own personal comedy of manners coming together in one space. It's too rich. Come on, Lynnie, when do we leave?"

Harold and I arrived at Art Nouveau promptly at 7. April had put my name on the guest list, but we weren't sure how to sneak Harold in. I agonized about it, but Harold simply strolled up to the

172

reception table and gave his name, "Fine," while he looked past the greeter like he was profoundly bored. Copping a glance at the list while the greeter checked the names, Harold tugged at the slightly too short blazer he had borrowed from Jonathan.

"I don't see…one minute…oh, yes, here you are. It was out of alpha order! Enjoy yourself, Dr. Fine."

"Dr. Fine?" I snickered as we wandered to the bar.

"You have not heard of me?" he asked, assuming an accent that sounded strangely like his Bubbe impersonation. "I speci-a-lize in multiple personalities." He became Harold again. "Seriously, do you realize how many Fines there are in the city of New York? The odds of someone with my last name being on the guest list were pretty good."

There must be one caterer in all of Manhattan who just does art openings, because no matter where the gallery and who the artist, you can always count on the same brand of cheap white wine that tastes and smells suspiciously like Heinz vinegar and the same bland water crackers with unripe Brie. Harold grabbed a plastic cup and a few broken crackers, but I passed on everything and pulled him after me to surf the crowded gallery.

Jill's *Power Series* sculptures stood out against the stark whiteness of the gallery walls. From the lush wooden vulvas of the 1970s that spoke to women reclaiming their sexuality, Jill had "progressed" to a series of cold metal sculptures, numbered 1 through 25. Each one was fashioned from a length of thin metal tubing that wrapped around and back on itself in a hideous twist, ended in a knob, and was polished to a dizzying shine. I saw some guests checking their hair and teeth in them. The card Claire had sent me did not misrepresent the sculptures: They were, in fact, twisted penises. Harold, my expert on all things phallic, confirmed it.

"Sheesh," he said. "What is it with this woman and genitalia?"

I could tell that quite a few gallery-goers were startled that Jill's hiatus from the art world had produced nothing more interesting than a bunch of gnarled penises. I overheard words like "ordinary" and "simple." But others were pronouncing the show "brilliant" or "full of energy," including April, whom I backed into while we were both vying for viewing space in front of *Power #5*.

"Such a bold statement for these postfeminist days," April was saying to the college-aged woman next to her who was scrupulously taking notes on a stenographer's pad. "Man hating in the '90s is outré, but...ow! Oh...Lynn! Lynn! Karen, you must meet my associate, Lynn Woods. This is Karen Kopek. She's doing her honor's thesis at Barnard on Jill. You'll definitely want Lynn's opinion — she's a lesbian."

Harold choked on a sip of cheap wine, but I remained unfazed. At cocktail parties April had outed me to everyone from Gloria Steinem to Mayor Giuliani, and by now I took it in stride. I assumed she flaunted me as her lesbian associate because it made her look tolerant and hip. As far as I was concerned, this was just one more nail sealing the coffin on my career with April.

Within seconds of greeting me, April was flitting toward Susan Faludi with open arms. "Susan! It's been *forever!*" April must have decided she didn't need me as a date after all. She just needed someone to dump poor Karen Kopek on.

"She's fabulous," Karen remarked in awe as she watched April glide away. "I can't believe I'm meeting all these famous people. I feel like I'm *living* Women Studies 101."

"Let me introduce my associate, Harold Fine," I said. "He's gay."

Harold and I laughed, but Karen didn't catch the joke. I could tell by the way she stared at me with one eyebrow slightly cocked.

174

Then she very seriously opened her notebook and scribbled something down while she asked my opinion of Jill's show.

"That's *L-y-n-n*," I offered, peeking over at her pad. "*L-e-s-b-i-a-n.*"

Poor Karen Kopek! My last quip sent her over the edge, making her hurriedly mumble "Pardon me" and head in the direction of Judy Chicago.

"You're shameless," Harold said with a smirk.

"Anyone who doesn't get my jokes deserves it," I said. My eyes made a rapid inventory of the room. "I don't know about you, but I've seen enough. Ready to go?"

"Oh, no, you don't. Claire has been across the room watching you for the last five minutes. Don't deprive me of this, please." When he nodded toward the far corner of the gallery, though, I didn't see her, because that side of the room was brimming with celebs.

"Oh, my God," I gasped, "there's Yoko Ono."

Harold — who as a kid had preferred the Rolling Stones to the Beatles because they had more of an "edge" — was unimpressed. "So let's go introduce ourselves."

"And say what? 'I loved your dead husband'? I don't think so."

Harold suggested we star-spot in earnest, and I joined in the game. He found Phil Donahue and Marlo Thomas (not difficult; Harold and Phil were among the small handful of men there), but I was much quicker and better at identifying famous feminists like Carolyn Heilbrun, Marilyn French, and Kate Millett than he was, and Harold never liked to lose. So he gave up and instead tried to study the sculptures more closely, looking for hidden significance. "It must be here somewhere," he insisted.

"I don't know, Harold," I said, neither softly nor delicately. "I'm not sure there's any meaning to this so-called 'ahrt,' beyond 'Genitals worked once, so let's revisit them.' "

I smelled a trace of sweet perfumed oil behind me — where had I noticed it before? "Lynn!" Everyone seemed to be calling my name in a short gasp of surprise. I turned to see Claire in a midnight blue sheath that hugged her curves like Michelin tires on a wet road. I started to take her hand in a mock-friendly gesture, but it was otherwise occupied: Jill Womann was monopolizing it.

"I'm sorry my latest work seems meaningless to you," Jill commented with a taut smile that looked like she'd just had a big gulp of her own wine. "I see it as having layers of meaning, but you seem to focus only on the most obvious."

Maybe she wasn't trying to be rude, but I felt I'd just been told I was too simple to understand her work. I felt hot blood rush to my cheeks. "Oh, the meaning is clear," I shot back. "What I don't understand is why you couldn't sculpt one twisted penis instead of twenty-five."

And this brashness on not even a sip of wine!

"They're metaphors," Claire inserted icily.

"Yes, I realize that," I said defensively. "But is there a difference between the metaphor of, say, *Power #6* and *Power #7*?" I pointed to two virtually identical pieces of contorted tubing.

"Lynn, don't embarrass yourself," Claire said. "Jill, I'm so sorry, but I warned you what she can be like."

I remembered Jill's haughty assertion that she made it a policy not to discuss ex-lovers with current lovers. She probably remembered it too, because she averted her eyes and quickly excused herself from our circle. I was deeply disappointed. I had this sudden picture of myself going down in a blaze of glory, trading insults with Jill Womann at her own opening.

"You should go," Claire directed in a monotone. "Harold, it's nice to see you again."

It felt like a rerun of our mediation session, with me getting in a few slam dunks, Claire leaving abruptly in a blur of color, and me left feeling dejected instead of victorious.

"You may have gone too far this time," Harold suggested, shaking his head seriously. "You could still go and apologize."

"No, never mind," I insisted.

"I've never seen you like this, Lynnie," Harold commented as he followed me to the door. "I know you have a sharp tongue, but tonight you could have cut through metal tubing with it."

"So it wasn't as much fun as you hoped?"

"I just pray I don't turn up in that Barnard honor's thesis as the homosexual friend of the strident *l-e-s-b-i-a-n*."

As we passed the reception desk, we overheard a white-haired gentleman insisting, "But I *must* be on the list! Dr. Ira Fine..."

"Let's get out of here and get something to drink," I said, snickering. "My head is throbbing. Let me just run to the bathroom first."

The women's rest room was as sleek and minimal as the rest of the gallery, all bright white tiles and lots of shiny chrome that reminded me of Jill's sculptures. There were only two stalls, and one was marked OUT OF ORDER with a sign hand-printed in calligraphy. I bent over to see if the other was occupied and spotted a pair of stylish black slip-ons beneath the door.

In the mirror I checked my face and waited. I looked angry and tense, and I tried to relax my facial muscles by exercising my jaw. That made me notice my teeth, which were clean because I hadn't touched any of the crackers or cheese. I pushed some stray hairs back into place.

Then I waited. And waited.

I thought I heard a deep sigh or a sniff from behind the stall door, so I tapped lightly on it. "Excuse me, is everything okay in there?" I didn't really care how "everything" was in there; I just wanted the occupant to know she was holding me up.

To my shock the door opened and I saw Jude sitting on the toilet lid, her face streaked with tears.

"Lynn!" she said through a stifled sob. "Am I glad to see you! Could you lock the outer door so no one else comes in?"

I flicked the lock on the door obediently and leaned against the frame of the stall. "You look miserable. What's going on?" Amazingly, seeing Jude in so much pain dissolved my anger toward her. She seemed so vulnerable and alone at that moment that my bitchy side — the one that wanted to ask, "So where's Lexy?" — went into retreat.

"I don't know why I came here," Jude bawled. "It was a *huge* mistake. Jill has obviously moaned to all her friends that I'm not the daughter she hoped for, that I'm a postfeminist no-talent or something. I can't tell you how many people have asked me what I think of Katie Roiphe and if I'm friends with her! And then April seems to have told everyone she had to fire Jill's poor incompetent daughter. The ones who aren't grilling me about my politics are patting me on the back and asking me if I've considered becoming a bicycle messenger. You know the worst part? I couldn't even do *that*. I grew up in Manhattan, and I never learned to ride a fucking bike!"

I crouched down in the stall opening and tried to think of something comforting to say. But the only thing I could think of at the time was, "Harold and I are getting ready to split. Wanna join us?"

She tore off some toilet paper and blew her nose vigorously into it. Her nose was red and dry, and her eyes looked as if she were having an allergic reaction to something, maybe her mother. "Are you sure?" she asked quietly. "I mean, I'd like that, but you have to be sure."

"I'm sure," I said, and honestly I was.

Harold and I took Jude to a trendy wine bar just a few blocks from the gallery. They served every wine you could imagine and almost as many brands of beer. We reveled in the number of choices.

"Thanks a lot for inviting me out with you," Jude sniffed. "I really needed a friendly face."

"Well, you got two for the price of one," I said.

"I didn't expect you to even talk to me after Fire Island and, well, Lexy and everything," Jude said. "I know you're pissed. But I can explain that, really I can…."

Harold looked extremely uncomfortable, like it wasn't all that entertaining to be in the middle of other people's dramas. I held up a hand to stop Jude.

"No need," I said in such a gracious way I surprised even myself. Harold cocked an approving eyebrow. "We're all adults. Let's all give each other a big fat break."

Jude was visibly relieved, and I felt a rush of pride course through me. Hey, it wasn't so hard to be generous to an ex-lover after all, even one who had wounded my ego. If I could do this, was it possible that some détente was attainable with Claire, the real heartbreaker?

Well, I didn't want to carry the grace thing too far. *Start small,* I thought. *Start with Jude, then see what happens.*

"Why didn't you bring Lexy to protect you?" I asked. Jude

glanced at me furtively, waiting for the trap to snap shut, and Harold's eyes registered the same apprehension.

"She's working," Jude answered slowly and cautiously.

"Oh, yeah," I said. "Friday night."

Both Harold and Jude looked like they wondered what locked room I'd shoved the real Lynn Woods into. Maybe I, instead of Dr. Fine, was the real specialist in multiple personalities.

"So," I continued, sipping my California merlot, "give us the dish. Tell us every gory detail about Jill Womann et al."

"Yeah," Harold jumped in, "don't leave anything out."

It must have been then that she realized the water was safe, that the shark that had snapped at Lexy Friday morning had in the interim been magically defanged. Jude talked and complained, while Harold and I inserted sarcastic quips about Jill and April and everyone else we hated. We moved from the bar to a table, ordered food, and kept up the flow.

Jude explained her seeming self-sabotage in not reporting to her job or calling April to quit. "I just couldn't take it anymore," she admitted. "I know it's not very responsible, but if you had to work with that woman day in and day out, you'd understand. I went a little crazy. I should have never taken that job in the first place."

"I understand completely," I said.

"April's like this insidious poison gas," Jude said, her face wrinkling. "One that you can't smell but that seeps into your lungs gradually until one day...*thump!*...you drop over dead."

"Great image," Harold congratulated her. "You could definitely be doing something better than working for April."

"I'm going to try to find something with no strings attached to my mother," she announced proudly. "Even if it means temping."

"And I'm declaring my independence from ghostwriting!" I

added, joining Jude's revolution. "We'll both leave April in the lurch!"

I didn't have much to drink, but I felt charged up anyway. Jude kept brushing against me in the way she had on our first sleep-over date. Around 10:30 Harold excused himself with a coy wink in my direction, and then the two of us were on our own.

"What now?" Jude asked shyly.

I was suddenly terrified of my own libido as I felt myself leaning into her ever so slightly. I was just a sweet kiss away from losing control and renewing the whole affair, the tormenting dyke drama of the last month. But did I really want to fall back into sleeping with Jude, who was sleeping with Lexy, who had been sleeping with me? *No,* I thought sensibly, *I'll defuse this ticking bomb.*

"It's still early," I said with forced enthusiasm. "Why don't we go to P.J.'s and visit Lexy?" I would drop her off with her new girlfriend, then head safely home. The rest was up to them.

Jude's face clouded for a minute, then cleared. It wasn't quite what she'd had in mind, but she probably figured it was good enough. At almost forty-one, I was still as naive as ever, because the next words out of her mouth took me completely by surprise.

"Then all three of us could go back to your place," she suggested with a sly grin.

Believe me, it was tempting. Sex à trois was something I'd never actually tried, but it had been one of the sexual fantasies Claire and I shared late at night when the lights were out. The third in our scenario was always someone famous and unattainable, like Jodie Foster or Ellen Barkin. The possible combinations of me, Jude, and Lexy, though mathematically containable, were suddenly staggering.

"Oh, Jude," I said with regret, "I don't think I could. It's just, I don't know, a little too devil-may-care for me."

Her face sagged again, and she leaned over and kissed me on the cheek with dry lips. "Then let's call it a night," she said, motioning for an oncoming cab. "I'm kind of beat anyway."

I held the door for her as she tucked herself inside the cab. "Thanks," I said sincerely, though I wasn't sure for what. I only knew that our dinner conversation had pushed me a step closer to severing ties with April.

"I'm the one who should thank *you*," Jude insisted. "You and Harold saved me tonight."

"I don't care who the fuck you thank," the cabbie remarked in a thick Brooklyn accent. "Just close the door and do it on your own time, okay?"

"Oh, keep your shorts on," I snapped. "Let's get together sometime, you and me and Lexy…just as friends." It was a moment of generosity that Jude probably saw through, because she smiled and pulled the door closed without another word except "Bye!" which came trailing out the window as the cab sped up the avenue.

The story isn't quite over.

Jude and Lexy and I would drop out of each other's lives as casually as we had dropped into them. That was what always happened in those kinds of affairs. There had been a string of women in my single days, Before Claire, who were just first names to me now and who had never tried to keep in touch, though we'd said very clearly, "Keep in touch." That's what many lesbians do — "keep in touch," have brunch once a year, peck each other's cheeks with sisterly kisses. I'm not sure why. Maybe we want something more out of the women we sleep with because we've all had our share of homophobic responses to the fact that we sleep with each other at all. Or maybe it's something less profound.

What I realized after I watched Jude's taxi zoom out of sight was that I might not need the connection with her or with Lexy, but I did seem to need something from Claire.

When I got home around 11 that night, there was a message from April. She sounded as ill-humored as she'd been over Jude's "disappearance," and I suspected what her code words meant. "We need to talk," she said firmly, the word "talk" underlined two or three times. "Needless to say, I was humiliated tonight by your behavior with Jill, and…just give me a call. We definitely need to talk." That time, "need" was punctuated.

She wasn't firing me by phone, but there was a firm note of warning in her voice. I waited until after midnight, when I knew she would have stopped answering the phone, and then I left her a cryptic message.

"April, this is Lynn. I have to quit the project," I announced calmly, boldly not considering what I would do next to make money. "I thank you for the opportunity, but it's just not the book for me."

Then I sat down and took out my pack of Marlboros. One by one I tore them in half and crushed the pieces into an ashtray. The last one I spared from torture and lit up, savoring the smoke as it curled above my head. When it was nothing more than a stub, I got out a spiral notebook and started writing a letter to Claire. I filled up four college-ruled pages, front and back, before I ran out of steam. I ripped out the sheets and left the edges raggedy. Folding up the letter, I stuck it into an envelope with a stamp and took it immediately out onto the street, dropping it into the mailbox on the corner before I could change my mind. It would go out in the 6:45 Saturday-morning pickup.

You'll forgive me for not telling you what it said.

"Hi, this is Lynn's answering machine. Leave a message."

"Lynn, it's April Ronsard. Please return all the material I gave you *right away*."

I listened to the final click that ended our arrangement — one more finality, another "breakup."

I don't think I expected more from April, but maybe I wanted some show of regret on her part, an indication that she would consider paying an enormous sum of money to keep me. Not that I'd stay, but I needed to be wanted, even by April.

But need wasn't forthcoming. After I played her message back a couple of times, I pictured April rubbing her hands together, calling Gloria and Betty and Bella to see if they knew anyone "suitable" for the assignment. April Ronsard wasn't a woman who looked back, and if I were her, I wouldn't either. I'd be too scared to see what I'd left in my trail.

I put out feelers for more work, and in the first two days alone, I was offered a plum ghostwriting job penning a series of multicultural picture books for preschoolers. The money could last for at least six months if I were frugal. It was tempting, and with a great deal of inner turmoil, I politely said no. Instead of writing other people's books, I wanted to try doing my own. For income I was looking for small editing assignments or copy writing to hold me while I finished my play. Though what would happen when I finished it, I wasn't sure. The market for lesbian plays wasn't exactly booming. Maybe I could *lose* money having it produced at a small venue in the East Village.

Since that kind of thinking is sure to produce writer's block, I took a deep breath and worked a day at a time.

I'm not going to lie and tell you the play wasn't autobiographical. I'll do what a lot of writers do and say it was semiautobiographical, even though whole scenes and dialogues were lifted directly from my life and the lives of people I knew. I found myself greedily copying down entire conversations, not worrying if so-and-so or who's-it would mind if I appropriated their words. Sometimes I felt more like a scribe than a playwright, but I remembered something that a novelist friend told me years ago.

"It's all material," she said, and she didn't mean bolts of cloth. She meant that life feeds the creative process, and it is the writer's ability and willingness to illuminate mundane parts of life on paper that is, in fact, the essence of inspiration.

Well, maybe she didn't mean all of that. But I do.

Since I had no other work, I wrote every day at the computer. I wrote and highlighted and deleted and moved and searched-and-replaced and wrote again. I spell-checked. I located synonyms in the thesaurus, substituted them, then returned to my original word choices. I wrote again. I did a word count. Seven thousand eight hundred and two, and L.J. Woods, aspiring lesbian playwright, had written each and every one of them.

And then it was finished. When the last page was written, I went back to the title page and deleted "A Play in Three Acts" and substituted "A One-Act Play."

It was short, but it was mine.

In the thirteen years we'd known each other, Harold and I had always been together on our birthdays, though with other people around, and it was a little funny to be alone with him in a softly candlelit restaurant that catered to intimate evenings. Our waitress kept smiling knowingly at us as if we were a heterosexual couple. She spoke only to Harold, until he decided to set the record straight, so to speak.

"Look, we're gay," he said, and her eyes widened and her cheeks reddened. "Homosexual *friends*. Okay?"

"What are you, now, Mr. Gay Pride since you came out to your parents?" I smiled as the waitress backed away from us.

"I can't believe how lucky I've been," Harold said seriously. "My parents are handling the whole thing really well. Seems I waited till the perfect time. They told me they were too old to lose any time being angry with me or bitter."

"So if we can all just hold on until middle age to come out to our folks, things might go more smoothly for us," I laughed. "How's Bubbe doing with the news?"

"She mostly wanted to make sure I was well."

"Sally Jessy's done AIDS."

"That would be my guess." Harold fished under the table for a bag and lifted it close to the candlelight. "Before I forget, my mom and dad sent you something."

"You're kidding!" I said with genuine surprise. "They must be really relieved to be rid of the shiksa."

"No, Lynn, they know you're important to me," Harold said. "I told them only a really good friend would help me the way you did."

I ripped open a small, soft package with a gift card signed "To Lynn. From Mr. and Mrs. Ben Fine." Inside was a smooth leather wallet, men's style.

"That's so sweet! I can't believe how sweet that is."

"They were going to give you a lady's wallet, complete with a built-in change purse," Harold explained. "But I told them I thought you'd like a man's wallet better. They both raised their eyebrows, but in the end, they gave in."

Next Harold handed me a flat box wrapped in *Looney Tunes* birthday paper. Right on top, Daffy Duck was spraying out, "S-s-sufferin' s-s-succotash! Have a happy birthday!" The card read, "A-cruising you will go, a-cruising you will go.... I wish you all the fun that life has to offer! Bunches of love, Harold."

Inside, under a wad of tissue paper, was a software program called "Internet Starter Kit." Harold knew I wanted to get on-line but was too technology-shy to find out just how to initiate it.

"You can meet people," he offered. "Talk to them on-line before you ever see them face-to-face. It's brought dating into the twenty-first century."

I made Harold stand up so I could hug him and plant a few kisses on his cheeks. "I adore you," I gushed as our waitress, looking *really* confused, brought our wine to the table.

Claire remembered my birthday, although several days late. She probably remembered it on the actual day and then mailed her greetings. In my self-pitying way, I imagined her going to the office, checking her appointment book, and wondering why the date seemed so familiar, until some hours later, before she met Jill for dinner, she realized the significance of July 15 and mailed a card on her way home.

Claire's card had a wispy bouquet of flowers on the front and a brief note inside under an elaborately scrolled "Happy Birthday to You" — the sort of impersonal Hallmark that might be in a section of the card rack just down from "Wife," "Sweetheart," and "Friend," unofficially designated for "People Who Don't Deserve Even a Sappy Poem."

Dear Lynn,
Thanks for your letter. I also wish some sort of friendship were possible for us now, but I need to think about it. Congratulations on your new life. Hope you have a wonderful birthday!
All the best,

Claire

Amazingly, it didn't make me angry or sad. It made me feel blank, like someone had just erased the last thirteen years from the chalkboard of my life — all the elaborate calculations and higher mathematics of love and relationships that I had been toiling over.

In a situation like that, there's not much else to do but pick up the chalk — no matter how much it squeaks or how messy it gets — and start figuring things out all over again.

Scene 6 (revised)

As the scene opens ROBERTA *is sitting stage left on a plain metal folding chair, holding a messy stack of paper. She speaks directly to the audience.*

ROBERTA
This is all my recent E-mail.
[*She spreads the papers out and fans herself with them*]
E-mail has brought dating into the twenty-first century, did you know that?
[*Looking at the letters curiously*]
Of course, if you print them out, are they E-mail anymore? Or have you changed their nature? Are they really only meant to live for a fleeting second on a computer screen? Did these women really want me to save their messages for posterity?
[*She looks off to stage right.*
Spotlight on stage right, where E-MAIL WOMAN #1 *enters, dressed in a black jumpsuit with a hood hiding her hair*]

E-MAIL WOMAN #1

You sound really interesting. But could you tell me what you look like? I'm sort of a cross between Jodie Foster, Whitney Houston, and Gloria Estefan. Write me at dee-lite@girls.com.

[*She is joined at stage right by* E-MAIL WOMAN #2, *identically dressed*]

E-MAIL WOMAN #2

I'm up for some HOT, HOT screen sex…how about you? Hmm? Write me at babe69@datenite.com.

E-MAIL WOMAN #1

My girlfriend just moved out on me, and living here in Rock Valley, Iowa, I find it hard to meet people. I know you're in New York, but maybe we could work something out long distance? My E-mail address is hardplace@-prozac.com.

E-MAIL WOMAN #2

I feel we've clicked, just in a few days. I could really commit to someone like you. I know we've never "met," but please tell me I'm not alone in these intense feelings. XOXO, desperate@fusion.net.

[*Lights off on stage right.* ROBERTA *faces the audience again*]

ROBERTA

Maybe it's me, but I have a hard time working up any enthusiasm for cyberdating. I liked the old-fashioned kind, the 1980s kind. You saw each other across a crowded bar, and one of you stared the other one down, eventually working up the courage to walk over and introduce yourself. Or else friends set you up, you made a date over the phone, you picked a restaurant you both liked. One of you showed up with a rose in your teeth for identification. You made each other laugh. You kissed each other shyly and made another date. You tried not to think about how scary the whole thing was. You brought the U-Haul.

[*Sighs*]

Whatever happened to romance?

[*Lowers her head.*

Lights up on stage right. E-MAIL WOMAN #1 *stands alone with her hood down. As she speaks,* ROBERTA's *head lifts slightly*]

E-MAIL WOMAN #1

I know one couple who met through a personal ad ten years ago, and they're still together. I know two gay men who met cruising in the park thirty-three years ago, and they're going strong. And I know a writer who answered a letter from a fan and they ended up in love. I could give endless examples!

I believe that desire is a void we rush to fill up. And sometimes a miracle happens, and it doesn't empty out again. A lot of it is just luck and good timing. If you want to write, my E-mail address is constance2@magic.com.

[*Lights out on stage right.* ROBERTA *stares at the black space where* E-MAIL WOMAN #1 *was standing*]

ROBERTA

Luck and good timing? Luck and good timing. That's what a friend of mine once told me was the formula for success as a stand-up comic.

[*She looks back at the audience quizzically, then the lights go out*]

191

This isn't a fairy tale. Svati wasn't the one for me. After I revised *Chicken,* I called Svati up, with sweating palms and shaking voice, to drop the hint in a subtle way that I'd cleaned up my love life and there was a place for her in it, lucky girl.

Unfortunately, I just missed her. She left the downtown apartment she'd shared with Lexy at the end of July. The new roommate, Chloe, who reported this to me, didn't really know where she'd gone, though she thought she'd heard something about Svati unexpectedly picking up and moving to California to finish her screenplay.

"Wait, my roommate Lexy would know more. Do you want to talk to her?" Chloe asked helpfully.

"No!" I shouted, then lowered my voice. "No, that's okay. Thanks a lot."

Click, another ending.

Oddly enough, this one made me laugh. I half expected Svati to be the person who would save me from having to be alone. I convinced myself she might be the heroine of this story — smart, pretty, and almost thirty! — and yet she'd left town without even saying good-bye.

Maybe no one could actually save me except me.

"I bet she liked you too much," Harold offered. "I bet she was scared that if she saw you again, she wouldn't go, and she really, really needed to go."

"Right," I said skeptically, popping a movie into the VCR and sitting down next to him on the sofa. "You're such a romantic, Harold Fine."

"So are you," he observed, motioning at the screen with the bowl of pretzels. "I wanted to rent *Interview With the Vampire,* but no-o-o!"

"You act like I brought home *An Affair to Remember*! These are cartoons, for God's sake. All I want is a good laugh." I fast-forwarded to the *Looney Tunes* title "A Wild Hare."

"But this is a classic queer love story — Bugs Bunny and Elmer Fudd! Bugs is totally out of the closet, and Elmer still struggles with it," Harold noted. "He wants to; he's just scared."

I hadn't seen any Bugs Bunny cartoons since I was little, when I had loved them. My brother, Will, and I couldn't be budged from the TV Saturday morning when the hour-long *Bugs Bunny/Roadrunner Show* aired. I'd never imagined that there was a queer sensibility lurking just below the surface of my favorite cartoons. Now Harold and I were roaring as Bugs stroked Elmer's rifle, then planted a big wet one on his lips. I felt giddily happy, a 41-year-old kid.

"See, Elmer pretends he doesn't like it, but he's definitely intrigued," Harold pointed out as Elmer wiped away Bugs's smooch. "He'll walk away, but he keeps coming back for more."

"The story of my life," I said, with a crooked, self-deprecating smile, but I knew I was in good company. It was basically the oldest story in the book.

Paula Martinac is the author of two other novels, the Lambda Literary Award winner *Out of Time* and the Lammy-nominated *Home Movies*. Her nonfiction works include a young adult biography of singer k.d. lang and the forthcoming popular history *The Queerest Places: A National Guide to Gay and Lesbian Historic Sites*. She was the editor and chief writer for *The Lesbian Almanac* and *The Gay Almanac*. She lives in New York City.

Publications from
BELLA BOOKS, INC.
The best in contemporary lesbian fiction

P.O. Box 201007   Ferndale, MI 48220
Phone: 800-729-4992
www.bellabooks.com

CHICKEN by Paula Martinac. 208 pp. Lynn finds that the only thing harder than being in a lesbian relationship is ending one.
ISBN 1-931513-07-4 $11.95

TAMARACK CREEK by Jackie Calhoun. 208 pp. An intriguing story of love and danger.
ISBN 1-931513-06-6 $11.95

DEATH BY THE RIVERSIDE: The First Micky Knight Mystery by J.M. Redmann. 320 pp. Finally back in print, the book that launched the Lambda Literary Award winning Micky Knight mystery series.
ISBN 1-931513-05-8 $11.95

EIGHTH DAY: A Cassidy James Mystery by Kate Calloway. 272 pp. In the eighth installment of the Cassidy James mystery series Cassidy goes undercover at a camp for troubled teens.
ISBN 1-931513-04-X $11.95

MIRRORS by Marianne K. Martin. 208 pp. Jean Carson and Shayna Bradley fight for a future together.
ISBN 1-931513-02-3 $11.95

THE ULTIMATE EXIT STRATEGY: A Virginia Kelly Mystery. 240 pp. The long-awaited return of the wickedly observant Virginia Kelly.
ISBN 1-931513-03-1 $11.95

FOREVER AND THE NIGHT by Laura DeHart Young. 224 pp. Desire and passion ignite the frozen Arctic in this exciting sequel to the classic romantic adventure *Love on the Line.*
ISBN 0-931513-00-7 $11.95

WINGED ISIS by Jean Stewart. 240 pp. The long-awaited sequel to *Warriors of Isis* and the fourth in the exciting Isis series.
ISBN 1-931513-01-5 $11.95

ROOM FOR LOVE by Frankie J. Jones. 192 pp. Jo and Beth must overcome the past in order to have a future together.
ISBN 0-9677753-9-6 $11.95

THE QUESTION OF SABOTAGE by Bonnie J. Morris. 144 pp. A charming, sexy tale of romance, intrigue, and coming of age.
ISBN 0-9677753-8-8 $11.95

SLEIGHT OF HAND by Karin Kallmaker writing as Laura Adams. 256 pp. A journey of passion, heartbreak and triumph that reunites two women for a final chance at their destiny.   ISBN 0-9677753-7-X $11.95

MOVING TARGETS: A Helen Black Mystery by Pat Welch. 240 pp. Helen must decide if getting to the bottom of a mystery is worth hitting bottom.   ISBN 0-9677753-6-1 $11.95

CALM BEFORE THE STORM by Peggy J. Herring. 208 pp. Colonel Robicheaux retires from the military and comes out of the closet.
                                                ISBN 0-9677753-1-0 $11.95

OFF SEASON by Jackie Calhoun. 208 pp. Pam threatens Jenny and Rita's fledgling relationship.   ISBN 0-9677753-0-2 $11.95

WHEN EVIL CHANGES FACE: A Motor City Thriller by Therese Szymanski. 240 pp. Brett Higgins is back in another heart-pounding thriller.   ISBN 0-9677753-3-7 $11.95

BOLD COAST LOVE by Diana Tremain Braund. 208 pp. Jackie Claymont fights for her reputation and the right to love the woman she chooses.   ISBN 0-9677753-2-9 $11.95

THE WILD ONE by Lyn Denison. 176 pp. Rachel never expected that Quinn's wild yearnings would change her life forever.
                                                ISBN 0-9677753-4-5 $11.95

SWEET FIRE by Saxon Bennett. 224 pp. Welcome to Heroy — the town with the most lesbians per capita than any other place on the planet!   ISBN 0-9677753-5-3 $11.95

Visit
Bella Books
at

www.bellabooks.com